T0149268

T-Plates & Black Chariots

Kevin Jenkins

authorHOUSE®

AuthorHouse™
1663 Liberty Drive
Bloomington, IN 47403
www.authorhouse.com
Phone: 1 (800) 839-8640

Published by AuthorHouse 04/20/2018

ISBN: 978-1-5462-3889-8 (sc)
ISBN: 978-1-5462-3888-1 (e)

Library of Congress Control Number: 2018904946

Print information available on the last page.

*Any people depicted in stock imagery provided by Getty Images are models,
and such images are being used for illustrative purposes only.
Certain stock imagery © Getty Images.*

This book is printed on acid-free paper.

To Peige, Cheyenne, and Lulu

Patrick's Afternoon Delight

My mind is in a trance. My gaze is transfixed by the hazard lights of a box truck directly in front of me on Seventy-Ninth Street and Columbus Avenue. I watch the flickering red lights with tired eyes. Off. On. Off. On. My hands slide off the wheel and fall into my lap. The glowing clock on the dashboard of my vehicle displays 11:40. I've been on the road all morning since my first trip to Newark Airport, an early run at five o'clock. A spectrum of red now torments my vision when I rub my eyes with both palms. I think about those red lights, cautionary twin beakers that warn drivers to proceed with care. I think about how the underuse of those lights can be an occupational hazard on the city streets, when the irritating, unpredictable yellow cabs become hazards themselves, darting across traffic lanes on Park Avenue without so much as a warning to other drivers. I feel my rage rising and take a deep breath. I remind myself to relax, stay composed, and drive defensively to get through the day.

I think about my twin brother because he's moved to Georgia and hates driving in New York City. "It's like dodging three-thousand-pound bullets all day long," he says.

The rear passenger door of the black 2014 Toyota Camry SE sedan I'm sitting in abruptly swings open. Bitterly cold December winds briefly invade and disrupt the warmth of the vehicle. A very attractive young woman with dirty blonde hair coursing down an expensive, full-length, goose-down coat slides onto the black leather seat.

"Hey," she exhales heavily. She shuts the door, escaping the cold clouds rising from the car's exhaust. She closes the zipper of her jacket at the top and rubs her hands. I distinctly but quickly notice that she barely has anything on under her coat. I think to myself that perhaps she is still in her pajamas.

"Good morning," I reply. I use some momentum of energy, brought on by the rather sudden surprise of her good looks, to sit up with rapt attention in my seat. I get one of those cheeky, fake smiles from her. I manage to return a polite, if forced, smile because my neck still aches from my previous long airport trip.

I tap the "Arrived" button on the app loaded onto a small iPhone issued to me by Superlative, the gargantuan, worldwide, luxury ride-sharing company for which I work. I wince as I realize that I forgot to tap it when I was supposed to, which was when I first pulled up in front of her building. I became mentally sidetracked while I was waiting. I have to get used to the routine. There's certainly no lack of repetitive practice.

This amounts to practical exercise because I need to routinely get it right without thinking so that I can think about the dozen or so other things on my mind. The worst worries are my overpriced rent, the vehicle-lease agreement that I signed in desperation, child-support payments, and expenses like the E-ZPass balance that I must maintain in my checking account. Like the majority of economy-wage earners, I'm obsessed with how I can stretch the pittance of the balance left in my account to cover the week's expenses until the next welcomed automatic bank deposit. I ponder for a moment about what I can do to escape this life of driving on perilous New York City streets without colliding into one of those yellow ticking time bombs.

I imagine roadside bombs in Iraq.

I quickly slide my finger across "Begin Trip" on the screen, and the app on the screen does its automated task. It displays the name on the account, as well as the location name and address of where she's headed: the Sherry Netherland Hotel on Fifth Avenue. She is discreet enough to have entered the entry of the destination herself and not left it to me. This subtlety could mean either she is cautious about the drivers who provide her services, or she's in a hurry. It could also mean both of these things. I prefer it when riders make their own entries; it saves me the trouble of doing it before the rides start.

"Is the temperature of the car okay for you?" I sing this rehearsed line with as much engagement as I can muster.

"Mmm-hmm," she purrs, already lost to what's outside the window.

I have learned to routinely ask this question. It strategically sets a positive tone for the trip and usually indemnifies me against a bad rating, because a good rating must be kept to maintain satisfactory status as a driver with Superlative. The rating appears in decimal form next to the customer's name, similar to a university student's grade point average, from 3.5 to 5.0. A score of five points, or stars, is exemplary, whereas any score below that is subject to immediate termination with no questions asked. The ratings system is a rather peculiar and explosive subject depending on which driver or rider offers an opinion. It brings to mind the universe of things subject to the prejudicial tastes of the city, each one more capricious than the other. Some riders find it natural to prematurely inform the driver what rating they will bestow upon them after a satisfied trip.

I've become quite alarmed about rumors of drivers getting an unsatisfactory rating over discretionary issues such as an unkempt car or possessing a poor command of English. It is common for drivers to misjudge a location due to a faulty GPS locator on the app, resulting in riders having to walk a short distance to board. This causes some wrath in their reviews.

I find the rating system particularly problematic because it seems statistically skewed. Only perfect 5.0 reviews raise my rating, whereas any infraction causing a loss of a star immediately weighs down my rating. The system seems built to cause ratings to sink more quickly than its rules show a propensity to allow ratings to rise. This design appears to embody Superlative's intention to ensure exemplary driver conduct. Drivers get to rate the riders too, and some riders do have a bad rating—but bad rider ratings are free, to a large extent, of any punishable consequence.

I study the woman in the backseat with clandestine glances as she tilts her head back on the comfortable seat headrest and stares dreamily out the window. *Her discretion is with good reason,* I think to myself as I glance again at my iPhone. It displays the name Patrick, who is the likely sponsor of her excursion downtown from the Upper

West Side. I notice that Patrick also possesses a relatively high Superlative rating of 4.8.

As mentioned, I find having to type in the destination before embarking or while in traffic slightly irritating. Some riders who claim to be in a hurry don't put in the destination entry beforehand, which seems rather counterproductive on their part.

I sneak another quick visual snapshot of her in the rearview mirror. She's attractive in a way that makes me curious about Patrick, the man on the receiving end of this fetching afternoon delight. I'm embarrassed by my stark objectification of her, and I shake my head and tell myself to focus on navigating the traffic. I fail to realize that she's caught me staring at her. She is young, but she is definitely not a minor. My eyes shift away to survey the traffic behind us in order to shake the trail of her possible suspicion.

Part of the mandatory class given by the Taxi and Limousine Commission is spent in recognizing possible sexual exploitation among minors. Even if the case was clear, I hypothesize, and a desperate expression seeking help could be gleaned from her radiantly moonish face, who am to I stop the inevitable march of the world's oldest profession? I wonder how much of my observation of her is idle symptom searching, and how much is just sheer sexual fascination.

We go across the Central Park transverse at Seventy-Ninth and fly down Fifth Avenue. We finally reach the front of the entrance of the Sherry Netherland Hotel, and I pull over and put on my emergency hazard lights.

"Okay, here we are," I say with a sigh, tapping "End Trip" on the app. "Have a good afternoon."

"Thanks, you too. So how do I look?" she purrs after a pregnant beat.

"I'm sorry?" I blink as I swing around toward her.

"How do I look?" she repeats, this time speaking with slow deliberation.

I turn my head and see that she has opened her full-length goose-down coat far enough for me to see, and there she is, in all her tantalizing glory, draped in expensive lingerie. My mouth freezes open as my eyes drop and survey the sultry length of her. I give her a thumbs-up. I am the roadkill purged in her dazzling headlights.

"You look like you're gonna have a good afternoon!" I stammer before lapsing into an embarrassed chuckle.

She laughs too. "Do you need me to sign anything?" she asks, buttoning her coat.

"Oh, no. It's all taken care of," I say quickly, already trumped by her.

"Thanks." She smirks.

"Thank you," I respond with a heavy emphasis on *you*.

"Bye now," she teases.

A coat sleeve from one of the doormen embroidered with the Sherry Netherland emblem tugs the door open.

I realize later that I should've stopped staring. I'm also pretty sure that she and Patrick had a lot of fun on that cold December afternoon.

Work Becomes War

I t's November. I toy with the idea of becoming a luxury black-car driver to supplement my dwindling income. Instead of merely boosting my income, I figure driving could turn out to grant me some reprieve from a tenuous work environment.

I work as a tennis instructor through the winter at an indoor facility just off the Major Deegan Highway in the Bronx. I'm well above proficient, I thoroughly enjoy it, and most days don't seem like work. The bread and butter, or profit center, of the tennis club consists of catering to rowdy, rambunctious children after school. In essence, the club is a glamorized babysitting service masquerading as a tennis academy, save for a few exceptional kids who aspire to be competitively ranked juniors or collegiate tennis players.

But we are fast approaching the warmer months, and there is a feast-or-famine mindset among all the tennis staff because rainouts, sleepaway camps, and family summer vacations during the summer outdoor season threaten to reduce tennis lessons, which means less earnings. It becomes a stressful way to make a living.

I am attempting to turn a small cadre of private junior lessons into good young players when a "new policy" at the club is implemented. One of the stipulations of this new policy means that for every private junior lesson I teach, the tennis club also needs to have that same child enrolled into an hour-long, "mandatory junior class" with any club tennis instructor.

I begin to sense some dirty politics.

Soon, the new policy becomes an effective but stealthy way for the club to gain influence from, and ultimately control of, all private junior customers. The club maintains that it's a way to limit instructors from monopolizing the limited court space, but the more experienced instructors knew what the policy really means. It's a coup, a way to hijack private lessons that have been imported by the new teaching staff.

It reminds me of when Ronald Reagan dismantled the air traffic controllers.

The parents who can afford it adapt to the policy, but most parents don't see the reason to increase their costs to play, and my little book of business drastically reduces as a natural and intended consequence. Surprised at how well the policy is working, the club offers me their newer clients for a while, but at a markedly lower wage per hour. With my lessons obliterated, I am now at the club's unbridled mercy. To make matters worse, the pay raise I had requested earlier in the year now seems completely unwarranted to the club's owner.

In a great sense, it is a microcosm of the broader low-wage service or gig economy, an economy caving in on itself as large corporations enjoy fat profits by top-loading management compensation while simultaneously suppressing wages of salaried workers. In pretty much the same way, the management at the club flourishes, and the hourly pay instructors are left hanging out to dry. After months of steadily building customers, my polite request for a raise is passed from one of the owners to a manager, who passes it to another manager, who passes it to the head instructor, who promptly quits before the "new policy" is introduced. This confirms my suspicions and paranoia about the deep deceptiveness of the management of the club.

Tensions and accusations begin to develop within the instructor ranks. Tennis instructors of black and Caribbean descent start to voice long-held assertions that they are being placed on back courts, barely visible to customers, whereas younger instructors who are "culturally easier on the eyes" are conveniently placed on the show courts despite their diminished proficiency and experience.

I begin to lose sleep and my appetite. I feel marginalized, bitter, and resentful. I internalize everything and obsess about how to cover myself financially. We become rats on a proverbial sinking ship. I read articles about how workplaces everywhere seem like the *Titanic*.

"These people just don't fuckin' care about us," Omar, a Ghanaian instructor, emphatically tells me while waving his arms in the air.

"What do you mean?" I ask. I am baiting him, urging him to audibly and plainly spell out what I've already acknowledged.

He sucks his teeth with a great smacking sound and continues. "All dey care about is banking fuckin' money, those greedy bastards!" He sucks his teeth again and with a mighty swing strikes a tennis ball hard and high in the air, down to the last of four bubbled indoor courts. The thud of the ball crashing into the strings of his racquet echoes in the bubble.

I offer him a wry smile and motion with my hands for him to be calm, turning the palms of both my hands downward. I know Omar can be excitable, and we are commencing a class of after-school children aged eight to fourteen. They are already within earshot of us and raucously sprinkling onto the courts.

I decide to hatch a deception of my own. I will, as a necessity, never again offer up transparency to an employer about what I am up to. I realize that the company that feeds me lies and claims that I'm part of a family doesn't care about what ultimately happens to me. This becomes not only my reality where I am employed the reality everywhere for virtually every salaried worker in the United States.

The next morning, I begin to fake symptoms of a phantom back ailment. I'm also encouraged by e-mails that I get from Superlative after an initial e-mail inquiry. The head tennis instructor asks for two weeks to prepare seasonally before leaving the club. He is summarily ordered to leave immediately before the end of that day's business. The tennis club's heightened appetite for heavy-handedness makes my motives even more clandestine. I become sullen, quiet, and moody. I cancel my Saturday seasonal lessons of two particularly spoiled, bratty teenaged hedge-fund babies—lessons that were lucrative to the club. I do this to serve notice to the club that I don't particularly care about getting their new business anymore. I know the club has me heavily invested into that expensively scheduled time slot, and it costs them a pretty fair amount of credit back to the hedge-fund parents, one of their best customers.

The club then begins to substitute all teaching time slots for collegiate tournaments or rented corporate events. Holidays and four-day weekends become unwelcome occasions for me because it means no court bookings for the period, and my earnings suffer even more as a result.

Work becomes war.

I am playing with fire, and I know it. I become frustrated with a game that I'm bound to lose. With my savings dwindling, I decide to pay Superlative a walk-in visit on my next free opportunity.

Superlative is the leading transportation technology company in the world, worth an estimated forty billion dollars before even so much as an initial public stock offering. Superlative operates in almost every major city and stands virtually unopposed competitively. It is also interesting for me to learn that Superlative considers itself, on the whole, a technology company rather than one that supplies transportation. I'm quite sure that is the company's expressed intention in order to avoid certain regulatory obligations for each major city in which they do business. The automated technology application of the company, or "killer app," is said to already have transformed the industry completely and permanently, and everyone is buzzing about the company. This to the complete chagrin of the traditional yellow and green taxi companies who operate from a seemingly obsolete (at this point) medallion licensing model. The growth of Superlative is rumored to be monstrous, and Superlative seems to be enjoying the perks of being a leader of the industry.

So sublime in simplicity yet so vast in its operations and execution, Superlative makes people wonder why they didn't think of the idea first.

I'm also pleased to find a job where my earnings don't seem vulnerable to any downturns in the economy.

Cast into a Superlative Net

I read somewhere that Queens, New York, was the livery car driver's capital of the city. Of each of the city's five boroughs, more livery car drivers live in Queens than any other borough of the city combined.

I'm standing in a long line of new applicants outside a dingy, one-story warehouse building of the Superlative East Coast Corporate Headquarters in Queens. The sky is a dullard grey, and there is a slight drizzle when I shake out my umbrella and enter the cramped complex. Candidates are ushered into a neat room the size of a middle school classroom, with rows and rows of small metal chairs. The chairs face a small theatre screen with an introductory video playing, but the audio can't be heard unless you pick up one of a stack of padded wireless earphones that are sprawled across an adjacent table as you enter the room. I pick up an earphone, quietly sit down, and adjust the earpiece over my head. The video is in the middle of the presentation.

"Whether you do one trip a week, or twenty trips a day, we are confident that Superlative is the best place to drive and make great money! Get started today. You can get activated online and use your own phone, or you can get activated here. Bring your vehicle documents in and pick up your Superlative iPhone! Don't have a car? No problem! Check in with our financing desk for easy terms. Top partners on the Superlative system are already earning over two thousand dollars a week, and that number is only going to grow as we approach December!"

The video loops around to the first half, and I listen intently. I look around the room and see various lines of candidates at various tables with Superlative staff helping new members sign up, process the needed insurance and licensing documents, and get locations for car financing.

Everything seems so automated and efficient.

I am impressed with what I see, and it becomes the answer for which I am searching. My chest heaves with anticipation as I impatiently survey an event chain in my head. Okay, I only need a taxi and limousine license and a vehicle, and from what I can already notice, obtaining the vehicle won't be an issue. The credit needed for the leasing of the vehicle is granted as a condition of joining as a Superlative driver, and the black car leasing dealers are all noticeably lining up to be affiliates of Superlative.

The new applicants (including me) who busy themselves at this table or that can smell the new money to be made in the coming months.

Despite this buzzing of commerce, I notice something. All the friendly faces behind the desks efficiently digital processing, stamping, reviewing, and speaking so patiently are young people. They all seem just out of college, almost as if they all share the same first apartment. They also all seem to be not originally from New York City. They seem similar to the squatting hipsters who hang out in the East Village or Williamsburg. The small but smart labor force seems perfectly manufactured and exported. They all are very neatly communicative and articulate. They seemly hail from places like Seattle, Delaware, Boston, and Connecticut. I can hear no grizzled ethnic types, and there are no almost minorities working.

My eyes narrow into an expression of suspicion.

I eavesdrop on a sun-baked Bangladeshi man as he is ushered to a back counter. A slightly older than most bearded man behind the desk is patiently explaining policy with a stern countenance. "I'm sorry. Your app was turned off because your rating has dropped below a three point five."

The Bangladeshi man leans forward and makes a gesture with both hands, suggesting lack of comprehension. He emits a grunt. "Eh?"

The manager clears his throat uncomfortably. "Yes, um, your rating. It's not good anymore. It's below acceptable."

"So I get accept to go back," the Bangladeshi driver says in his best broken English.

The manager realizes his task. He raises his chin, blinks his eyes, and speaks firmly. "No, your app has been turned off. You have to turn in your phone to me, now."

There is a pause. The driver's eyes turn first away and then downward as he reaches in his back pocket for the phone and slaps it on the desk. He gathers up his backpack to make a hasty exit.

"I'm sorry. Good luck to you," the manager says as the man storms out.

I feel a disdain washing over me at the manager's feeble attempt at condolence to a man who now has to promptly find another means to support himself and his family. I think about how continually rude or undisciplined the Bangladeshi driver had to have been to warrant his own termination. I silently assure myself that the event I just witnessed will never happen to me. It also occurs to me clearly for the first time that Superlative uses technology to silently control and exploit a vast, capitulating workforce.

The Poor Dead Guy in the Toilet

One Hundred Twenty-Fifth Street and Lexington Avenue on Harlem's East side is peculiar because it's a place where the indigenous, roaming regulars are stuck in time. I was a small child when veterans like my Uncle Lester, strung out on heroin or methadone, were streaming back in the United States from the Vietnam War. I distinctly remember their drowsy mannerisms, the upright nodding, and the freakishly unpredictable body contortions of the addicts as they milled around, high on substances, waiting in their tour-weathered army jackets for heaven only knows what. I noticed how small and contained the once large population seemed, now gone like the mighty bison.

I wonder if this abject milling of idle people is a perfect indication to prospective apartment hunters of a terrible neighborhood. My delicious fascination of that area is further evidenced by a stop I make into the corner McDonald's for lunch. A large man wearing a navy security officer's uniform stretches out his arm and places the back of a swollen, meaty hand in front of me I as I attempt to enter the bathroom. "Where you goin', sir?" he quips.

"Thought I'd use the restroom first," I respond.

"You gotta show me proof of purchase."

"Oh, I see. I'm guessing you must have some stories about what goes on in that bathroom," I say knowingly as I turn to head back toward the serving counter.

"You have no idea," he bellows. He laughs and almost spills his McDonald's coffee. He seems eager to tell the story. I wonder how often he is asked.

"Check this out," he says, following me to the serving counter. He whips out a cracked iPhone from a large pocket on the front of his uniform shirt. "This one was just last week."

On his phone screen is an image of a man face down in the bathroom toilet. He has seemingly expired from a heroin overdose. It is a morbid sight. The spectator in me is unabashedly fascinated. Equally fascinating are the noticeably swollen hands of the security officer himself. His outsized, swollen, and scarred hands reveal the symptoms of his own past heroin use, of a community of users who routinely find the veins needed for heroin dosages by plunging a syringe into the backs of their hands.

I wonder if perhaps the security guard sees himself in the picture of the poor dead man in the toilet.

The Poor Guy Living in the Toilet

A professional woman in her late forties climbs into the back passenger seat on Fifth Avenue, headed for Newark Airport. She fields me cordially when I ask my temperature of the car question and alleviates my initial sense of alarm. Her brown hair sits in a fluffy, short, bobbed haircut, revealing a youthful but squarish face. She curls the corners of her mouth in a look of sincerity and is open and frank.

"Oh, good. You seem like a normal driver," she says. "My job takes me back and forth from the airports a lot. About a week ago, I was running terribly late for a flight when this driver, an Indian fellow, asks me if he can stop so he can use the bathroom. I ask him if it can wait because I had to board in twenty minutes. He proceeds to complain and moan about it the entire time. I busy myself with some documents, and all of a sudden, I notice the faint odor of urine in the car! The guy is relieving himself inside some sort of bottle or container while he is driving! I was never so shocked and disgusted. I guess he figured he was gonna just go right there. He didn't care that a woman was in the car. Meanwhile, my face is pressed outside the open back window like, 'Bleah! Get me out of here!' Needless to say, I declined when he offered to get my luggage out of the trunk."

I shake and howl with laughter at the story and firmly grip the steering wheel to keep from crashing into the side rail.

Drive a Car. Make Ten Grand This Month

I proceed into the large building just east and beyond that forgotten heroin corridor, where the Department of Motor Vehicles is located. The first task of my clandestine mission is to register and modify my driver's license to a class E license, which is as easy as filling out a quick form. For a small fee, I am now certified to operate a vehicle and carry passengers.

Master Cabbie is on the second floor of a dull, obscure, unkempt, brick-faced commercial building on a bustling Jackson Avenue in Queens. It's nine thirty in the morning, and I'm running late for the first of three eight-hour, all-day classes. The building is surrounded by a horde of men who are at first glance mostly foreign-born, dark-skinned men. There is of course the occasional white, salty-haired Russian, Ukrainian, or Eastern European sprinkled in the crowd. Peculiarly, all are largely representative of the many countries smoldering in violent winds of upheaval, and likely some indirect consequence of American policies that nary one can understand with complete lucidity—policies that are above and beyond any attempts to comprehend aside from the next plate of food for each of the respective families. I walk quickly past them as they huddle for a quick cup of coffee before class. Some are smoking, and some are pacing nervously. Many countries are represented by the assortment of languages being audibly spoken: Croatia, Haiti, Montenegro, Pakistan, India, Somalia, Yemen, Syria, Ghana, Nigeria, Turkey, Morocco, Lebanon, Togo, Bangladesh.

I think about how we are all linked to one commonality, completing the requirements for a taxi and limousine license, so that we can get on with bettering our lives. I muse about how all of us, financial underpinnings aside, must make an investment of time and limited resources for the purpose of some collective financial stability.

We all seem to be perfectly and conveniently served up into the dragnet of the Superlative labor force under a tenuous but lethal, low-wage economic landscape.

I squint my eyes at the sun high in the partly cloudy sky, and I unsling my black messenger satchel bag from my shoulder so that it stops pinching my neck. I open the heavy door, squeeze inside, and hustle up the creaky wooden staircase to register.

"Good morning, cabbies, I'm Tom. Everybody sign in?" our instructor bellows as he stomps commandingly into the large classroom. He wears a lumberjack-style vest, jeans, and heavy steel-toed black combat boots. I'm reminded of my middle school years, with the same mixture of morning bright sunlight and low-quality fluorescent lighting. He clasps an attendance list, and his staccato voice booms out our family names in alphabetical order. His boots scrape the floor heavily and authoritatively as he paces the room. The voices speckled about the large room fall silent, sensing his mood. My anxiety to find a seat in front and to the left becomes a regrettable mistake as his temperamental tone emanates to the back of the classroom and my ear chambers at the same time.

"Muhammed!"

"Here, sir."

"Mustafa!"

"Yes, here."

"Saliph?"

"Here."

If a family name cannot be pronounced, he bellows the first name and then asks for a clear pronunciation. This happens often.

"How do you say your name?" is frequently followed by "Where are you from?"

Tom is noticeably both smart and curious. He is not smart in the way some people would generally think of, in some overrated academic sense. He's smart in an intuitive, raw sense.

"What you will learn in this classroom will help you out there on the road, so listen up. Hey, could you shut that window a little back there?"

Responding quickly, an Algerian in the back of the room complies. Tom slaps down books of street maps unto a desk in the front corner of the room.

"Rule number one—hey, listen up and be quiet in the back there, or you are free to leave," he crows.

The room falls deadly silent again. Heads turn and crane in mocking complaint of the audible transgressors, sitting in the back of the classroom. Tom pauses and waits in uncomfortable silence. There is a nervous cough.

I immediately recognize what he is doing. He is establishing claim to what will be his domain for the next three days, and he's vanquishing any would-be challengers for his undivided attention. It's a smart opening agenda.

"All right. Rule number one: Once your customer gets in your car, your car belongs to them. It is no longer your car for the time being."

A South African student raises his hand to contest the statement. "What do you mean? They are not paying the note on the car." The class laughs.

"You're from Superlative right?"

"Yes …"

"I remember you. They sent you back to this class when your rating fell too low, right?" The student doesn't answer. "That's why you're right back here. How many people are signing with Superlative? Raise your hand. Keep 'em up high so I can see, please."

A comfortable majority raises hands. I do too.

"How many doing yellow?" Very few hands go up.

"How many are doing Bloomberg's greenies?" Even fewer hands go up.

Tom chuckles at his own sardonic labeling of the green cabs, the cabs that circulate the outer boroughs of New York City.

"A lot of money he prolly made, creating those greenie cabs." Voices murmur and heads nod in agreement.

With a captive audience, Tom grandstands now. He is the quintessential portrait of the veteran cabbie of twenty-plus years. As he speaks and paces in front of us, a keychain filled with keys dangles and clangs, bouncing from the loop in his jeans. He has a cutting, gnawing cynicism that one might suspect from being a cabbie for as long as he has.

He pauses and raises an eyebrow, almost as if an idea has just come to him. "You ever hear the saying that the customer is always right? When they want the AC on, you'd better put it on. They want the radio on? Put it on. Same with the windows, the seat, et cetera. We'll cover more on customer service the last day. But you'll begin to get a feel for customers as soon as they step into your cab. If they want to go to Javits Center, and you picked them up from the Radisson in Times Square, you'll know that they're probably in town for some convention, and they're probably late or pressed for time."

"Why?" a voice yells.

"Because there is a good chance they didn't account for the time it takes to get through traffic, because the location of their hotel is close."

I feel like a complete plebe. My face feels warm, and I begin to feel anxious. I think about why the hell I would want to be a professional driver. Then I go over the stakes again in my head.

Tom grabs a stack of maps and drops them on a front row table to be distributed. As this happens, a large Pakistani man comes through the door and attempts to scurry to a far side seat near the entrance. He is sweating profusely.

"Hey, you. Where you goin'?" Tom booms. Then he vehemently shakes his head. "Uh-uh, no. Go home. Come back tomorrow and show up on time."

The large Pakistani man throws up two big hands in quiet protest. He pauses upon sensing the annoyed countenance on Tom face. He grabs his jacket and quickly walks out of the room. An Indian student shakes his head in disbelief. The latecomer now has to make up the class next week. I glance at the floor, sympathizing for the Pakistani man.

"That was pretty cold-blooded right?" A man seated next to me whispers. I nod my head. He is American and has the all-American look: bright teeth with a stubbled face. Expensive Ray Bans sit on top of his black hair. He possesses perfect, indigenous English, which is noticeable in the context of the class.

He introduces himself to me as Kent as he hands me a map. I take one and pass the others along. Tom has left the room to escort the latecomer. There is an unintended break in the class.

I introduce myself to Kent, and we clasp a quick handshake.

"Yeah, I'm not doin' the Superlative thing," Kent tells me. "Taking 20 percent of what I'm making is robbery. Hey, you live in the city? Maybe we could talk about sharing a yellow."

Kent is already networking and is all business. He didn't notice my hand up among the prospective Superlative drivers.

We sit down for a drink after class in a bar across the street from Master Cabbie's. I discover that Kent is an "actor slash screenwriter." The bar is how we both like it as far as bars go: an unpretentious, understated dive with good jukebox selections and decent beer on tap.

"I like the idea of Superlative," I say a half octave above Billy Joel's "New York State of Mind."

"Really?" Kent says, nodding his head to the selection. "That 20 percent hurts when it adds up, man."

"It might, come to think of it. So how and why did you come to all this?" I ask. I let the chilled Corona hit the back of my throat. I taste the bitter lemon slice that I've stuffed into it on my tongue before it washes in with the Corona.

"Pretty sweet gig for anybody in the arts that has to get to auditions," he says. "You?"

I tell him about how I hate the politics of the workplace, and how I'm looking forward to having my own hours. "Having my own vehicle for a change will be convenient for me to get around," I add.

I secretly hope he doesn't sense that I am bullshitting him. Telling him that I'm getting into the Superlative life to escape that I am vulnerable in my line of work might strike him as some sort of pathetic desperation.

Kent launches into one more attempt to dissuade me from Superlative and convince me to share the bounty of a yellow cab enterprise.

We touch on a debate. The subtlety of our debate is light but respectful, which I find refreshing among two men who are simply seeking a better place in the world, with no ax to grind and no egoistic goal post to move. The liveliness of our debate increases with each round of drinks.

"I just have to pay a garage fee for the day, and the rest is mine," Kent explains, "You can't beat that."

"That may be so in the short term, but you have to fight with other yellows to find fares, sometimes swerving spontaneously in traffic and risking an accident to pick up fares. If I have the Superlative app, I already know where my customer is, and from what I hear they're everywhere. Plus, I don't think I can deal with that antiquated meter. Digital automation and GPS is so much better. There's also no favoritism from some shady guy at some base doling out the most lucrative rides to his favorite drivers," I argue.

Kent raises an eyebrow. "For technology, you'd trade 20 percent of your income?"

"Yep," I mutter proudly.

"Then good on ya. Godspeed, mate," Kent says raucously in his best drunken Australian accent. For inebriated sport, we mock slurred English, Australian, and South African accents for the good part of an hour. I silently yearn for the freedom and simplicity of my old college theatre classes.

We have a last toast for the evening. I have another cold bottle of Corona, and he has a shot of whiskey.

I stumble out to the seven train on Jackson Avenue, almost tripping on the stair step entrance. However drunken my state, it doesn't go unnoticed that Kent climbs into a Superlative car to head home to Union, New Jersey.

I'm back at Master Cabbie's on the fourth and final day. I stare down intently at a written examination administered by the Taxi and Limousine Commission (TLC), the regulatory agency that governs and enforces driver education. This is what Tom has done his best to prepare us for. The examination consists of thirty questions challenging English proficiency, and another fifty questions covering street and borough geography as well as TLC rules and regulations. Our class has been combined with a group of students from another class I haven't seen before. A map of the five boroughs of New York City is on a chalkboard in front of us, covered up by a dingy projection screen that has been pulled down over it. I'm slightly distracted because there are five proctors for the examination. Tom sits in front of the classroom and is joined by a colleague instructor from the other class, a stout, powerfully built Haitian in his late thirties wearing dark jeans, a matching jean jacket, and a Rastafarian cap that holds in place a mass of snakelike dreads. There are three people from the TLC, two young African American females and a Latino male. The whole affair seems like overkill—until I notice that the Latino male ominously wearing handcuffs. I suspect that he is from the enforcement division of the TLC.

Two men are thrown out of the room for cheating. They are told to wait outside and do so without protest. I find the test ridiculously easy and am almost finished. I proofread over my answer sheet, which has an appearance similar to the standardized testing that the city schools conduct, in which circles are filled in with a number two pencil on a computerized sheet. My desk squeaks as I squirm out from underneath it, and I move to the front of the room. Tom takes my completed sheet with an expression on his face like he knows I'll pass. The results, he explained earlier, will be known tomorrow and will be disclosed by phone.

"Congratulations, and good luck to you," he whispers, shaking my hand.

I grab my black messenger bag and my jacket and creep out of the classroom. Kent is waiting downstairs, having finished before me. "I'm kind of pissed that I studied for a lot of questions that never showed up," he says, stomping out a cigarette.

"Some of the people are really struggling. And the ones who got caught cheating!"

"Yeah, I know. I just kept my head down when that happened."

We both pause. There is a realization between us, one that had previously been taken for granted. At that very moment, we are glad to be indigenous Americans. We are also in full understanding of our language and our advantage. I can't imagine crossing open deserts of the Sudan or Morocco to get to places like New York City, London, and Paris, only to fail an examination arguably designed to be linguistically deceptive to foreigners.

Kent and I say our goodbyes, and we promise to keep in touch and meet up at a good bar somewhere in the city, sometime in the future, to discuss our relative progress. There is an unspoken, subtle, competitive undercurrent that we both sense: ourselves against each of the men who were our classmates scrambling for a place in the industry, a place in the world. We small talk for a few minutes more, and he reveals to me a recent development: His fiancée is pregnant. I can barely contain my feeling of emotion.

"I got a feeling you'll be one helluva father!" I laugh, slapping him on the back.

"I'll save a cigar for you next time I see you," he replies, beaming.

On the seven train back, I stare out the window at the Long Island City urbanscape, noticing the familiar greenish hue of the Citibank building. On the side of a bridge is a huge sign that I can just make out in the distance: "Drive Superlative. Make $10,000 this month."

I think about how I am one of an infinite number of the struggling underclass, one of the proverbial spawn moving upstream to some unknown place a safer distance away from the constant threat of poverty, personal ruin, or destitution.

The Precariat Class

I remember reading somewhere that the French call their young generation the Precariat, or the precarious generation. It is a fitting word by definition, meaning "something not securely held in position, dangerously likely to fall or collapse" according to Google. It also means "uncertainty or dependent on chance." I think about the delicate act of trying to switch occupations and simultaneously not jeopardize my living conditions. My savings have dwindled and my bargaining position as a worker is weak, so I can't afford to disclose to my current employer what my position is, although my position to them would be presumably replaceable.

Five hundred dollars down, borrowed from my beloved godmother, gets me behind the wheel of a late model Toyota Camry SE on a rainy Saturday afternoon. I drive it off the leasing lot of American Leasing, a livery dealer on Ogden Avenue in the Bronx, after signing a leasing contract. The largely Dominican staff do so much business that they barely notice me. The place is crowded with prospective black car operators. I waste no time in picking out a vehicle with the lowest mileage on the lot, 16,500 miles. I do not opt for the larger vehicles because the fuel costs don't seem immediately sensible nor feasible. The car hums beautifully down the cramped, double-parked streets. I become immediately aware that there are for hire Camrys, Highlanders, and Explorers everywhere—T-plates, recognizable by the T being the first letter of the livery license plate issued by the TLC. I feel the clock ticking as soon as I hit the Major Deegan Highway. There is an ominous lease payment obligation of $369 per week, and so I am motivated to hit the ground running without buyer's remorse or looking back. I now feel anxious and manic, and time seems to speed up. I look at the dash and see that the tire pressure indicator is on. I make a mental note to stop by the tire place in Washington Heights.

I am a neophyte, and I learn quickly because I have to or else it ends up costing me money. I sleep late this cold weekday morning, which I thought would be a luxurious perk of being a Superlative "partner," but I find out that sleeping late is a heedless liability. The best hours to work of the limited daytime hours are between 5:00 a.m. and 9:00 a.m. because morning rush money is always there. That and long trips to the airports (LaGuardia, Kennedy, and especially Newark) are optimal because the longer trips take in the most money. Superlative surge pricing does the rest.

Surge pricing happens when a jump in demand for Superlative vehicles causes the price of a ride to increase incrementally, sometimes two to three times the normal pricing. This happens like clockwork according to a mysterious but brilliant algorithm that seems to kick in when it's rush hour, snowing, or raining, or when there's extremely heavy traffic.

I have missed that advantage this morning, and so I'll compensate by extending today's schedule a little further into the evening.

Daytime driving becomes noticeably different than nighttime driving. Daytime hours seem to be more stressful, with everyone running late and looking to cut through traffic. Crosstown client appointments, babysitting, apartment showings, morning school bells, and last-minute shuttle flights clutter my short memory during the daytime rush. I'm thrown headlong into the pulse of the city such that soon I cannot remember the first ride.

Nighttime driving is easier, especially after 8:00 p.m. The perpetual machinery of the city slows down and grinds to a pause before picking up again. The driving becomes more enjoyable because time isn't as punitive. The Superlative sweeping tentacles serve the metropolis dinner reservations, nightclubs, and corporate functions.

At two weeks in, I am keenly attuned to small cues. My default radio setting is the Lite FM music, set to barely over a whisper.

A tense rider asks me to turn it off. He isn't on a call; he is simply in one of those moods. He searches his iPhone e-mails. I listen to snippets of him sending and receiving early work messages for the day's business. His jet-black hair is slicked back as if he was in the shower not less than fifteen minutes ago.

"Temperature of the car okay?" I ask him.

"Fine," he grunts.

I am most attentive during times like this because I'm fully aware that my rating could take a dive for even the slightest rider irritation.

On an earlier ride today, a woman got on at Amsterdam Avenue, close to Lincoln Center. She had the typified countenance of the Upper East Side maternal type, with a short and neat conservative bob haircut. At first I thought soccer mom, but no, she was too stuffy, too uptight. She has the terse, stern mouth that's slightly wrinkled from a chronic scowl. The Superlative app indicates that she is going eastbound, across Central Park.

"I've just had surgery, so could you not go over any potholes?" she asks.

"I'll certainly do my level best." I hope my disingenuousness isn't detected.

I wince as I picture the inevitable mounds, craters, and raised manhole covers along the Eighty-Fifth Street transverse going crosstown through Central Park. I spend a good deal of the reduced speed ride secretly fuming over the audacity of her request.

I love the Upper West Side. The residents seem friendlier, more talkative, and more liberal with their "newer" dollars and easy attitudes. Some insist on tipping, even though it is not permitted by Superlative.

"That's the thing that bugs me," one woman says before getting out at a popular Amsterdam Avenue restaurant. "Why gratuity is not thought of as proper for a personal service suggests to me a lack of conscience of thought for drivers out here busting their asses. I am being subjective, though. I used to work in the service industry." I do not disagree with her when she shoves a five-dollar bill at me.

I also learn to not care much for the Upper East Side. I find residents to be on the mean-spirited side. They are also notoriously cheap, with their old, conservative co-op buildings and more traditional but restrictive East Side trappings of decorum. I soon make it a practice to do all that I can to avoid turning the app on along its streets, preferring instead to scuttle back across the Eighty-Fifth Street traverse off of Fifth Avenue. This becomes my favorite route back to the Upper West Side, and I don't mind turning off the app for an extra five to ten minutes. In the beginning, frequenting the East Side much too cavalierly is responsible for my initial rating drop from 5.0, never again to return to that summit in ratings.

On one evening, an attractive brunette mom in her thirties loads her two cherubic blonde toddlers into the backseat. She immediately seems stressed out, exhausted, and short on temper from dealing with the toddlers, who seem to be two to three years old. She manages a wave goodbye to her playdate colleague, another attractive young blonde mom whose toddlers are already nestled in their carriages. In caution to moving traffic, I have opted to stay on Lexington Avenue rather than make the turn inside her block, because the GPS pin in my app has located her on the corner. The Superlative app leaves the option to the rider of being able to call or text me for specific instructions, such as directing me to make a left turn on Lexington inside her block. To my detriment, the brunette mom doesn't exercise the option.

"I wanted you to make the turn inside the block going east!" she barks as she snatches the door open. She is barely audible over her daughter's screaming, probably over the announcement of a good time halted. I scramble out of the vehicle and attempt to fold up her double Maclaren stroller so that I can squeeze it into the trunk.

"Oh, I'm terribly sorry. I think the pin is a little off getting your location." I suspect that the only harm done has translated into a few extra steps toward the corner where I was parked. I am terribly mistaken.

"We could have walked home quicker than you came. We're just going around the block, and now you're taking us an extra block!" she whines, snatching the reins of the Maclaren, closing it with deftness and shoving it into the trunk.

I think, *How'd she?* for an instant. I mastered the proficiency of that stroller move when my own daughters were toddlers. I've lost the knack, whereas she has become the Michael Jordan of the Maclaren stroller.

I climb in and swipe "Begin Trip." Indeed, the screen's destination shows that she is just going around the block to Third Avenue.

"You really didn't have to go this way," she continues.

I read somewhere—I forget where—that completely assuring a customer, owning up, and being accountable to any mistakes or misgivings is paramount to great customer service. "You know, you're absolutely right," I announce. "Let's get your little ladies home. I can just turn off the app and take you the rest of the way, no problem at all."

This becomes a trademark staple of mine, to immediately turn off the meter, "end the trip," and finish the ride per any misunderstanding or any directional mistake made.

"Well, okay, but you're missing my point."

I swipe "End Trip" silently as a counterpoint that I'm doing so only to address her point. There are some people who take any commiseration as permission to dig their heels in deeper. I sigh.

"Temperature of the car okay?"

I chalk up her frustration as not being about me. In my mind, she is already out of the car, and I make a bold outside play at protecting my rating. I take a deep breath and promise myself a successful, smooth ride to make up for this one.

Of course, the next day my perfect 5.0 rating is gone.

Partner of the Precariat Class

I'm rubbing my eyes in early morning while behind the steering wheel. Evenings at home are starting to blur together. I can hardly recount the quick dinners, the phone calls to my daughters, and the brief news before crashing to bed. The fatigue burning underneath my eyes begins to accumulate. I do enjoy the calm quietness of early morning. There is a vast hue of blueness in anticipation of the impending sunrise. It is four o'clock in the morning, and I'm snaking down one side of Manhattan's skeleton on the West Side Highway. These are thoroughfares of the city that I repeatedly find myself on over and over again. The Major Deegan, the Saw Mill, the FDR, the 9A or West Side Highway, the Joe DiMaggio.

I begin to be concerned about several contemplative matters since I've commenced driving. I check my Superlative app, and it indicates that I need to head farther downtown, supposedly where the demand is. The first issue I contemplate is how my schedule has a glaring and pivotal effect on how much I earn. It becomes crucial to drive certain hours in order to meet gross expenses and attain an operating income. Here I am, making a consistent point of beginning my day at 5:00 a.m., and my chances of coming out ahead operationally still depend of the luck of the cumulative ridership. I can complete my day at 5:00 p.m. on a good day, but the good days are few. The longer the rides, the more optimal the earnings. Rides of short duration are completed begrudgingly and are not welcome.

I've stopped work at the tennis club save for weekends, and word among the staff is that management is not pleased with me. I'm not particularly concerned. They didn't pay a livable wage, and I did give them fair warning that I would seek other options. I am somewhat anxious about Superlative being the chosen option. Like many others, I am rolling the dice on Superlative.

My first weekly check totaled eleven hundred dollars, wired directly into my bank account. Not only that, but the process is extremely automated, along with all my documents. Two days before the check hits my account, I am sent a Superlative summary detailing useful statistics: the hours I drove versus the busiest hours, the average dollar amount that I earned per hour versus the top drivers, the average time spent on the road versus the other drivers. There are also ratings statistics. My rating last week was 4.81 versus the top driver ratings average of 4.78.

Below the statistics, it reads, "We hope you find this information helpful, and that it guides you to an even more successful Superlative experience."

I find this a very acceptable and satisfying indication of the possibility of things. It took my former employer three weeks to set up my direct deposit account, and another week for me to get paid. I am always suspicious of employers, and how I get paid is a major sign of how my employer values me. Do I have to go looking for my money once I've earned it? My old employer at the tennis club paid me fourteen hundred dollars every two weeks, and so I feel like I've inched ahead. They've also botched my biweekly payment three times. The amount of the check was simply wrong, and it was up to me to bring it to their attention and reconcile the amount, which means to me that they would cheat me if they could. I feel my senses sharpening with every personal debit and credit. Admittedly, I wasn't as focused on this as I needed to be in the past, and so now every stop at the gas station is scrutinized. I notice that I am reimbursed by Superlative for E-ZPass expenses for trips going out to the airports, but not upon returning. I begin checking my credit card statements with more regularity, glaring and grimacing with each debit expense like some old scrooge sitting at my kitchen table.

My instincts are raw and new, and some eyebrow-raising inconsistencies begin to show up. A week before I acquired my vehicle, I receive an e-mail that states, "Whether you drive a few hours a week or ten hours a day, we're confident that Superlative is the best place to make money."

> Directly underneath was a simulated payment statement that read, Payment Statement: Trip Earnings: $2,613.72, Miscellaneous: $10.00, Total Payout: $2,603.72

> This partner drove 60 hours and made $2,600.00 in a single week!

I am surprised that the 20 percent deduction by Superlative is not included. I smile at the convenient hidden deception produced by the e-mail. I am also both concerned and outraged by the "helpful" suggestion of a sixty-hour work week.

I note and fully discover another deduction called a "black car fee," which was not previously mentioned in the neatly packaged Superlative training videos. Although it seems to appear out of thin air, it amounts to a variable percentage expense each week, increasing as the amount earned increases. Sales taxes also takes a significant portion of the weekly gross, and its deduction is accumulated along with a daily leasing fee of $379 per week. I find myself happy to not have to deal with the complicated fees associated with the Taxi and Limousine Commission, such as livery insurance, livery plate, and base diamond card fees, all of which would amount to between two and three thousand dollars annually, depending on which livery base in the city a particular vehicle is associated with. I am content to pay the leasing fee to my base, American Leasing, who deducts this leasing fee before any other deductions by Superlative. There is also the expectation that in exchange for that seemingly usurious leasing fee, I should own the vehicle with the last of my 154 payments. I guess that's the cost of being the boss, or as Superlative would word it, a partner.

I remember one of Kent's drunken comments at the bar, affected with a South African accent, that was spot-on authentic. "See, eh? Superlative uses the term *partner* very loosely. I always thought that definitively, a partner in a business shares equally the revenues and expenses of the partnership. If one of the partners decides not to pay for some of the expenses, that ain't no partnership, eh? They're like a major league sports team who doesn't want to pay for its own stadium, eh? So they'll make you pay for it, eh? Superlative keeps all its revenues yet socializes out its expenses to a small army of drivers." I got his point, and there was no counterpoint.

I contemplate the additional discovered cost of Superlative technology. Somehow, it still beats wrestling with those noisy old taxi meters. I'm also knee deep in the Superlative lifestyle, and I can't possibly turn back now. Besides, with full black car associated expenses due, what would be the immediate alternative but to press on and hope for the best?

That Giant Sucking Sound

I t's early evening, and I need to gas and go to the bathroom. I am idling on Twenty-First Street between Eleventh and Twelfth Avenues, outside the art galleries in Chelsea, waiting on Craig. I have a calming expectation that the ride will be a smooth one because Craig has already entered in his destination, a popular sushi restaurant on Eighth Avenue in Hell's Kitchen. A tall, thin hipster type in effeminate skinny jeans gets in the car, greets me, and politely informs me that there will be a delay; he's waiting on friends. We wait ten minutes in silence while the meter runs, and we listen to 1010 Wins news reports of the latest ISIS bombings, with the volume barely above a whisper. I notice him sit up, and out of one of the galleries come his expected company toward the car: another tall hipster in skinny jeans and a Ralph Lauren shirt, and an attractive girl in her early twenties. She is not tall or angular enough to be a model, but her feminine beauty is far less innocent. I think of the *Maxim Magazine* brand of models, the kind of beauty that is a lot more common—and more sex suggestive to compensate for it. She's wearing tight-fitting, ripped jeans and a tight top cropped around her shoulders, drawing attention to the contours of her shapely figure.

"Hey, man, what's up," the second hipster says while climbing in.

"Temperature of the car okay?" I ask. The first hipster closes his eyes and quickly nods to me.

The girl is still in midconversation. "So, like, how was I supposed to know how much the Guild says I made last year? They sent me this thing asking me, and I have, like, have no idea. I hate tax stuff."

I begin to feel this strange sense, like the air is being sucked out of the car. She speaks incessantly, only pausing to hear reassurance or stale encouragement from the hipsters. She is dating and intimate with the second hipster. She is in from Los Angeles and was having issues with the key to where she was staying. Could she possibly stay with him until her round of auditions are concluded? Does he have a good tax person to help? She was auditioning for a part and ran into his old girlfriend, another actress who was auditioning for the same part. Does he know that she didn't mind or feel the slightest bit jealous or uncomfortable? She talks the talk that people ambitious in show business talk: loudly enough so that people in earshot who are outside of the business should be audibly impressed.

"You know, I really don't feel like hearing the news. Could you turn that off?"

I am listening to the news of a possible nuclear deal between the United States and Iran as I drive, but now my "rule number one" alarm has been tripped. That is my cue to say as little as possible and concentrate on the traffic. I look for every opportunity to step on the gas and shorten the trip duration. I take a silent but deep breath, anticipating the slow deflation of available oxygen in the vehicle for the remainder of the ride. I add pressure to the accelerator pedal, and the needles on the dash slowly jump to the right, aiding my call for help.

"Thanks," she huffs.

We fly down Eighth Avenue. I begin to immediately wonder whether this young actress has any talent at all, because her focus seems to be on how much attention she can garner rather than the internal feeling behind what she is saying. Forced listening reveals that the second hipster is "handling" her career.

We arrive at the restaurant, and I breathe a sigh of relief as I swipe "End Trip."

"You have a good day," she says in a mocking tone as she shuts the door.

For fun, I decide to google her from my Android phone while I watch her strut into the restaurant with her male entourage. She has gotten some acclaim from winning marginal beauty pageants in Arkansas, which led to a spread in *Penthouse*. She recently shot a commercial in Japan, which she is currently capitalizing on to propel her through this audition season. I feel miserable for the second hipster because he seems to be thinking a little too much with his private parts. I roll my eyes, check my mirrors, and step on the accelerator, merging into Eighth Avenue traffic and hoping that the next ride erases the memory of this one.

My Cold, Damp Business

The men's bathroom in Riverside Park, down the hill along Ninetieth Street, hasn't been cleaned yet this spring afternoon. I'm annoyed also that the door is ajar, exposing my cold, damp business, and there are no paper towels. There is the irritating sound of children playing noisily on the playground next to the park structure that houses the bathroom. It's irritating because there is only one urinal and one toilet. In the back of my mind, I keep imagining scenarios of children running in and out of the cracked door, holding the front of their trousers while doing the "I gotta pee-pee" dance and waiting for the strange man to leave. My nose wrinkles at the faint odor of urine and bleach. I sigh, wringing my wet hands out after running them in cold water and then brushing them against the backs of both my thighs to dry them. I take bathroom breaks like this with increasing regularity since I started driving. I'm certain it's because I'm gaining weight from a haphazard diet of meals on the run in the streets and the constant sitting in the vehicle. Bathroom breaks are not livery friendly, but I catch them as catch can.

I already have keenly developed my favorite emergency places to go. Along Riverside Park and Ninetieth, as mentioned; the Hippo Park off Ninety-Sixth Street; the River Run playground on Eighty-Fourth Street; and the Riverbank State Park on 145th Street. Parking is a hastening challenge if I am in dire need to go to the bathroom, but it's less challenging if I can hold it in and wait. If I'm in a place in the city where I can't make it back to the West Side to use a bathroom, I can usually get to the Lincoln Center Library on Columbus and Sixty-Eighth Street. I can get to the hidden public park for the wealthy alongside the Trump Buildings along Seventy-Second to

Seventy-Ninth Streets, or to the Park off the Queensboro Bridge exit on the FDR Highway if I'm stuck east. There's also a sharp right turn coming off of the Triborough Bridge along 125th Street if I really need to relieve myself quickly and am returning from one of the airports.

I briskly walk back to my vehicle parked on the corner of Eighty-Eighth and Riverside Drive, and I find an orange parking ticket stuffed in the windshield. I was deemed too close to a fire hydrant, and so now a $115 penalty will be deducted from my bottom line. I rub my eyebrow and think about other bills that I will be late in paying as a result of this. The city is an inhospitable place today. I snatch the ticket from between the windshield wipers, causing the fresh ink to smudge, and bend myself into the car. I slam the door hard in utter frustration. My eyes search around and meet the eyes of the doorman across the street, who has been watching my inevitable bitter reaction to the ticket. I am his morning's entertainment. The conspiracist in me wants to march across the street and ask him if he tipped off the patrolling traffic officer that he chats up every morning. My mood is foul. This city. This goddamned, selfish, cold city. I have the impulse to quit for the day. I am my own boss now, a "partner" at Superlative, right?

But I am only fooling myself.

There looms the ever-present weekly livery lease note from American Lease and all those incidental expenses. I am compelled to make my expenses and my living, like a gerbil in a wheel that is always spinning. I am the insect of a myth spun by the spider who created the web on which I sit, entangled. I sit silently in the car that owns me, staring at the shiny black steering wheel and the truth.

Two black livery cars pass by, turning south on Riverside. One has a passenger, and one is without. My stomach sinks and churns, and I wonder whether those drivers feel as I feel at this very moment, bound intricately to my vehicle and it to me.

I check the battery level of my Superlative-issued iPhone, and it's running out of juice. The battery life of the early generation iPhone turns out to very poor, and it's set upon a cradle close to me on the windshield of my driving side. That means I have to remove it from the cradle and place it in the front center in order to charge it using the vehicle's electrical plug, which is next to the stick shift. If my battery runs out of juice while I'm on an extended trip, the app will fail to calculate the trip cost to the customer, and I'll have to discount the trip to the rider. (That has already happened, and despite a long, smooth trip to Long Island City, a customer smelled opportunity and demanded a discount due to the battery failing.) I check the dash and find that my tires need air and my gas is low. The passenger carpeting of the vehicle is also filthy, and so I'll have to stop in to that gas station I prefer on Riverdale Avenue at the bottom of the hill, near 231st Street in Inwood.

I'm also hungry, having had only three apples and some slices of pound cake from the bottom of my refrigerator. I've become fiercely addicted to the two cheeseburger meal with fries at the twenty-four-hour McDonald's on Thirty-Fourth Street and Tenth Avenue. I like that place because it resembles the capital of a fictitious town called Cabbieville, with its parking lot chock full of livery and yellow cabs of all makes and sizes, a hungry population of like occupation doing what I do at some unorthodox hour of the day.

Although I've done a few good airport runs to Newark today, business slows down unexpectedly, and so I must work through some part of the evening. I've figured out that I need to gross four hundred dollars a day for five of the seven standard days of the full week in order to have a chance at earning a check for one thousand dollars after expenses.

I'm exhausted on weekends, and so my motivation to hit the road on the weekends is low. Besides, I have won weekend visitation with my daughters. Driving is out of the question compared to the intense Scrabble games when I'm accompanied by them. I begin to experience a pinching in my neck and lower back due to discomfort with the vehicle seating position. This is despite sitting on a pillow embroidered with the insignia from the popular boy band One Direction, given to me by my daughter out of loving concern upon hearing me complain about it.

In the back of my mind today, I'm also worried about a trip I took from Plainfield, New Jersey, earlier today. I missed an exit and had to circle back through some tolls, which probably put a good dent in my E-ZPass balance.

At times I feel some deep sense of isolation while amid the bustling life of the city. I am alone but not alone when madly circling the routes of the city. Like Robert De Niro's *Taxi Driver*, I often feel this sense of loneliness, moving around the city yet standing still at the same time, like a moving dock. There is a silent weight when so many people come and go, talkative in relatively measured degrees between each ride, and I am left alone at the day's end, pondering the influence of their humanity upon me.

Am I becoming more loving of humanity or more callous as a result?

I reach down into the glove compartment and pluck out a picture of my sorely missed daughters, the daily convenience of seeing them now lost to an untimely divorce. My motivation to get through today sharpens.

I Can't Breathe

My Superlative app buzzes a text to me: "Where R U?"
Delores has sent the text. She is in front of her building on
Eighty-Fifth Street between Amsterdam and Columbus,
on the Upper West Side, searching for me. She doesn't realize yet that
I am approximately five to six doors down from her. A Hertz box
truck coming down her street, which has been narrowed by double
parking, has forced me down the street from where she is waiting. My
back strains as I paw open my door and lift myself out of the car. I
wave to her, and upon seeing me, she irritably nods and grabs for two
metallic crutches on her stoop. I await the earful that I will get once
she reaches me. *Damn, here we go again,* I muse.

"Sorry about that. I got forced down the street a bit," I say weakly
when she reaches me, attempting to head off the impending and
inevitable complaint.

"Oh, that's fine. I saw that. That truck was not so nice."

I blow out a breath of relief with puffed cheeks.

Delores is a big woman in her forties, and she's sweating profusely
and wheezing from shortness of breath like she's just sprinted an entire
city block. I feel compelled to give her some advice and instruct her to
take a deep breath in through her nose and hold it for three seconds to
slow down her breathing, like I used to tell my tennis students. But I
don't dare. I watch her get settled in the back seat and close the door
after she hoists her legs inside with her impressive forearms.

"Temperature okay in the car?"

"No. It's a little warm in here. And could you turn the radio off,
please? I sort of feel like I should warn you in advance: I get very

claustrophobic and crazy in confined spaces. But everybody's a little crazy about stuff, right?"

I am immediately on high alert. Rule number one has reared its ugly head again.

"Oh, and could you not go so fast? I like to try to listen and see the traffic so that it doesn't get so close to us." I offer her a nod.

I find Delores difficult but friendly. She is a nervously talkative television producer on her way to the television studios on Tenth and Fifty-Ninth Streets. We chat about the well-known anchorperson who her colleagues work for who was just caught lying on air about being under fire in Afghanistan.

"Yeah, all my friends on that floor tell me how much of a horse's ass he is," she howls. "It was only a matter of time before his mouth caught up with him."

She then starts to talks about the African American man who was killed for basically selling loose cigarettes. "Yeah, did you hear about him? I really take that personally. I mean he was a *big* guy. Where was he going to run? I can relate to him because he has health issues due to his weight, like me. The cop should've realized that the guy can't run and was of ill health when they restrained him. And he kept telling them he couldn't breathe! I get the wind knocked out of me just going up a flight of stairs."

At a stop sign going down Columbus, she politely asks me to roll the seat forward.

"Listen, my poor mother was being harassed at one time by her neighbors over her property line. So I come over one day and yell out to her within earshot of her neighbors, 'That's okay. The camera surveillance people will be here tomorrow to collect evidence.' Point being, you have to take your power, and you have to get it from somewhere."

She stops talking and winces to hear an approaching ambulance siren. I reassure her of where the siren is.

"Thanks for spotting it. The voices in my head were going crazy. We all have voices in our heads. By the way, did you know that Spock was a sociopath?"

Dolores is just about to explain to me how this is so when we arrive at her destination, the television network studios on Fifty-Ninth and Eleventh Avenue. Some rides are interminably long. Here I was, dreading the trip at the beginning, and the trip turns out to be entirely too short.

A Game of Chicken

There is a small stretch of road in the Kingsbridge section of the Bronx that takes me from 230th Street to a route down Broadway toward the Broadway Bridge on 225th street. This is the bridge that separates Manhattan and the Bronx. There is a quick right on Marble Hill Avenue, past the assembled morning students of George Washington High School rambunctiously waiting to cross the street, and then a left on 228th Street past a Dominican Methodist Church. I fail to notice that there is a sign that indicates that drivers are not permitted to make the left on 228th Street between 7:00 and 7:30 a.m. As a result, I am sitting idle beside traffic in front of the blaring lights of a traffic officer in an unmarked Dodge Durango muscle car. I guess the vehicle is readily built for chasing me in case I decide to make a run for it.

"License and registration. Are you aware that there is a sign posted?" he asks me while beckoning with his fingers for my documents. He peers into my vehicle. "I could also cite you for not displaying your hack license number, which you are mandated to do."

"Oh. My company didn't make me aware that I was required to do that," I reply.

The young officer is clad in a Mets jacket and wears sunglasses with a six o'clock shadow. He has an aroma of deli coffee. He pauses and considers my words with an amused, arched eyebrow and an almost surprised countenance before taking my license and insurance documents and returning to his vehicle. While I wait for him to return with my ticket, I am convinced that this corner is a bonanza for officers who are behind on their monthly revenue quotas. I've seen people take this left daily at this time when there was no police presence. I am late again getting into the city to earn my day's keep. I've already had to vacuum the interior of my vehicle and get gas to last me for the next day and a half. This traffic stop has added to my misery for the day, and the infraction comes with a three-point penalty on my TLC license. It also occurs to me that although I am caught red-handed, even if I had sufficient grounds to dispute the ticket, I would lose out on a considerable amount of days pay taking the time it takes to defend the points. Luckily, it's my first offense, and I figure to let the points fall off of my "untarnished" record in a year's time. I take the ticket handed to me and stuff it in the center compartment between the front seats. I thank the officer with a sarcastic and contemptuous tone.

It is midafternoon, and I am still reeling from the ticket. I'm on Park Avenue and Eighty-Sixth Street, noticing the neatly manicured dividers in the middle of the street. I'm at the light against traffic, preparing to make a left turn toward Madison Avenue, when I see a huge truck approaching, its International insignia prominent on the large chrome front grill some meters away and coming toward me on the adjacent side. A yellow cab behind me blares his horn and urges me to make the left quickly before the truck gets to me, in effect asking me to play a game of chicken with the truck. I glare maniacally at the cabbie in my rearview mirror, an aging Pakistani fellow with white hair and overbaked skin. I stick my middle finger out my driver's side window and scream at the top of my lungs, "Fuck you!"

The truck barrels past us at an alarming speed. I open my window, seething and shaking with an anger that I have never felt before. I shake a middle finger at him again and yell at the top of my lungs, "Fuck You! What the hell is wrong with you? Are you trying to get me killed?"

The Pakistani cabbie glares at me, and I see his countenance change. He thrusts out two wrinkled palms toward me as if to simultaneously say "I apologize" and "Take it easy."

I'm still shaking angrily and glaring at him. To him, my life was an impulsive risk just for him to hastily catch another light or another fare. He drops his eyes, guns his engine, and accelerates around me. I decide to wait for the next traffic light to change. The cabbie narrowly beats the traffic light change as he accelerates across the intersection.

I feel a rush of dizziness, and so I make the same left across the intersection and pull over to the side of the road. I let out a gasp of air and blink my eyes. I feel the tension decompress in my chest and my shoulders. This becomes my moment of clarity. Up until now, I have been in a slight panic, reacting to the madness and the bullying horns on the city streets. Now, I will willfully ignore them and listen to the found voice of my own inner calmness. Who cares about all other driver motives and interests? They are not mine.

The New World Sweatshop

I awake out of a deep sleep from a night vision. In the vision, Superlative becomes an enormous labor innovation, so much so that the Superlative lifestyle is celebrated as ground zero for foreign-born males emigrating into the United States, a virtual never-ending stream of cheap labor. Many other forms of service labor drop far below it in terms of a livable wage. The Superlative life moves ahead as the definitive labor standard and is lauded as a way to earn a successful middle income, similar to union pipefitting work at the turn of the century. I shudder as I drag myself to the bathroom and slap warm water into my sleep-deprived face as I step under the shower head.

Is the Toyota Camry the sweatshop of the new world economy?

In the blue hue of early morning, my phone buzzes before I start up the engine. It's my updated weekly driving statistics, conveniently sent from the Superlative servers. My eyes quickly scan as I scroll down the screen. A bar chart suggests that I could have earned up to $464 more dollars this week had I adjusted my chosen hours. (This is all in relative random hindsight, I notice; it seems I only drove four of the twelve busiest hours.)

I read, "This week, drive *all* the busiest hours!"

I chuckle and shake my head. The Superlative propaganda machine is at it again, hard charging at its unsuspecting private army of drivers. No one can possibly know when the busiest hours will be, and so the prescription seems to be to drive every hour.

I scan the chart statistics again. My riders say that my driving warranted a 4.71 rating. "Unfortunately, your driver rating last week was below average."

I frown upon noticing "below average" is in red font.

"On the bright side," it goes on, "you received 86 five-star reviews out of 104 rated trips in the past two weeks. We wanted to share what some of the riders had to say."

"Excellent!"

"Very friendly and polite driver!"

I frown again. The unsatisfactory rating and the five-star reviews seem to be contradictory, furthering my theory about the skewness of any bad ratings.

I keep reading.

Trips last week: 79
2 weeks ago: 54
Top drivers: 73

Ha! Top drivers, eat it! I think to myself.

Hours online last week: 49.6
2 weeks ago: 33.9
Top drivers: 44.0

"Yeah, that's what I'm talking about!" I shout.

Fares per hour last week: $37
2 weeks ago: $37
Top drivers: $46

"Uh oh," I bemoan.

Acceptance rate last week: 91%
2 weeks ago: 98%
Top drivers: 96%

I skip over this with stern silence.

> Driver rating overall, current: 4.81
> Last week: 4.71
> 2 weeks ago: 4.71
> Top drivers: 4.86

My silence is prolonged as I finally read, "We hope that you find this information helpful and that it guides you to an even more successful Superlative experience. If you have any questions or suggestions regarding this report, please e-mail us at Superlative. com. Signed, Team Superlative."

In the early morning light, I remain on the side of the road, pensive yet filled with an indignant, mild rage that I feel in my throat pushing out with each hard breath. I decide to send a response e-mail. The timing of the e-mail causes it to be terse and prompt.

> Dear Superlative,
>
> I am a new driver for Superlative for the past several months, and I wondered if management would consider the following.
>
> This week I received 86 five-star rating out of 104 and still had an overall rating of 4.71! This is disconcerting and discouraging to me because:
>
> A. It suggests that the rating system may be unfairly statistically skewed to the downside.
>
> B. If my rating continues to decline in this way, my employment may or could be reviewed for termination should it reach below 4.5, as per your new partner manual.
>
> C. Favorable comments, although nice, don't help us to improve as drivers. Only observations of critical comments will help keep us from consistently doing the things that get us a less than satisfactory review. (Please check my review comments; I'm always courteous.)

Could someone review the fairness of the rating system or let us see the bad comments along with the good?

Also, could you strongly suggest that riders input their destination before starting the trip, or make it mandatory to do so? That way we are not typing in traffic or in traffic waiting for the address to route if the riders suggest that they are pressed for time (as they are more often than are not).

I smile and feel a relief at having my underrepresented say. I think about what the response might be, if at all, and how long it might take. I check my mirrors, turn the ignition key, and turn on the wipers, expelling a disturbing amount of bird poop from the windshield.

Chop Wood, Fetch Water, Become Enlightened, Chop Wood, Fetch Water

It's early afternoon, and I'm at escape velocity, having broken away from the clutter of traffic down Fifth Avenue just beyond the Apple Store on Fifty-Ninth Street. In the back are two young recording industry turks talking shop. We break away from the earlier traffic crawl only to be trapped in gridlock again. Having traveled this way at this time before, I'm sensing that it's unusual.

"Hmm," says one of the riders.

"Will ya look at that," says the other in a recognizable British accent.

As we pick up speed again, we come upon the cause of the congestion. Two yellow cabs have collided in the middle of the avenue, and the chassis of one has twisted into the other. The wheel of one of the collided cabs has completely caved in underneath. Both vehicles are uninhabited, and there are no drivers in sight, with exasperated looks waiting for a tow truck or police.

"Jeez, where are the drivers?" asks the first rider, craning his neck and peering behind us as we pass.

"Apparently they both took off," says the British rider.

"Unreal," says the first.

"Don't picture that happenin' in London," says the Englishman. "There'd be hell to pay."

The conversation turns to how in London, the driving occupation is perceived as a more serious and dignified endeavor than in the United States, and it is treated as such.

"Drivers have to take a rigorous test that they call the Knowledge."

"Yeah, an old friend back in school took it quite a while back. Tough exam. Funny about the attitude of the business here."

I find it decidedly unfunny as I eavesdrop on their chat, pretending to be distracted by 1010 WINS Radio playing on a low volume.

"Yeah, there you have it. Maintain an illusion of respectability, and then you preserve the industry."

"Like banking?" the other says.

They both laugh. One sighs humorously.

"Well, you know what they say."

"No, what do they say?"

"Chop wood, fetch water, become enlightened. Then chop wood and fetch water."

I'm struck sharply by the expression, and I burst out laughing which catches both the riders by surprise. "That's a good one," I say, compensating for startling the riders midconversation. "Can I use that one?"

"By all means," he says.

They get out at Fifth Avenue and Twenty-First Street.

"Oh, sorry, are you allowed tips?" one asks, leaning back into the vehicle.

"Well, no, not really, but if you absolutely insist," I cajole.

"I absolutely insist," he says, handing me a ten-dollar bill.

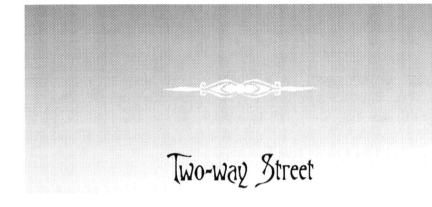

Two-way Street

I 'm sitting at a traffic light. I've swung around to return back up Madison Avenue when my phone buzzes again. I pull over to read it somewhere along Madison Avenue and Seventy-Ninth Street after I drop off a heavyset female tourist from one of the southern states who apparently was never told that she should never try to catch a Superlative car from the epicenter of Times Square. (It takes us forever to crawl through the afternoon pedestrian traffic.)

The e-mail is a response from Superlative:

> From: Debra @ Superlative, 1:37 p.m.
>
> Hello,
>
> I completely understand the concern about ratings. I smile at this first line. I remember that good customer service means aligning yourself with objections.
>
> If you feel that you were rated unfairly, although it can be frustrating, it will not have a significant impact on your overall rating or account standing.
>
> Your rating is the mathematical average of your last five hundred rated trips. Cancelled trips or trips that were not rated by riders have no effect. As a result of this being the average of so many trips, a single or even a few bad ratings will not have a major impact on your rating, especially as you continue to complete trips.

It's also a two-way street. Allowing partners to rate each rider also ensures all members of our community meet a high standard.

Thanks,
Debra @ Superlative

I feel some stark reassurance as I swipe my phone dark. Still, I can't help but remember the driver who was promptly dismissed due to a poor rating the day I first paid a walk-in visit to Superlative. I also start to think about how I can now begin to excuse myself from picking up drivers with a low rating because it's been made clear to me that there is a two-way street.

NYC Tip Jar

There are incredibly picturesque thoroughfares of the city on which I frequently find myself, one being the stretch of road snaking on Riverside Avenue and going past 152nd Street. It looks particularly gorgeous now, and I'm looking upon the magnificent lights that span the George Washington Bridge in the night sky.

I am dumbstruck at that sight this evening when familiar but dreaded flashing lights from an unmarked police vehicle turn on behind me, forcing me to pull over to the side of the road.

I find the image of two officers patting their holsters in synchronicity while approaching me from opposite sides acutely ominous. Through my fogging side mirrors, I observe the outlines of a male and a female officer.

"Turn off your ignition, please," the male officer commands.

"What did I do wrong, Officer?" I whine.

"Just turn the ignition off, and I'll tell you. License and registration."

I hand him my documents and wait in silence as the officers turn and convene at their car to check my plates. I feel numb as I stare down at crystals shining in the pavement, now slick from the fog, coming in over the adjacent Hudson River.

The female officer returns. "Okay, you were going forty-two in a thirty zone. Is there a reason why you were going at that speed?"

"I—really?" I clutch at my throat with one hand in astonishment while looking at the speedometer. "Officer, I could've sworn that the last time I glanced at the speedometer—and I check it a fair bit while I'm driving—it was right here." I point to a spot on the speedometer between twenty-five and thirty. "I didn't think I was *there*." I point to the forty mark on the speedometer.

"Well, some people make that mistake sometimes, and you probably didn't realize it."

The female officer turns and walks back to the unmarked car. I keep my head still and watch intently as the two officers convene again. The female officer moves her hands almost as if there is some sort of debate between them. I drop my head to my chest in frustration and exhaustion after a long day of driving the streets. I huff out a deep breath, feeling stress and a dryness in the back of my throat. I shut my eyes, attempting to imagine away and stamp out the consequence of my inadvertent transgression. I imagine the ticket dissolving in time like the others, and I figure on driving more conservatively than usual.

But this is New York City, and driving here means driving assertively, especially with demanding customers.

"Okay," the female officer says while handing me the ticket. "We cut you a break on reporting your speed on the ticket, so that you're not gonna be overpenalized by the TLC. Instead of citing you for speeding, we're bumping it down to failing to follow signage. That way you're also not subject to an immediate hearing. All right?"

"Okay, thank you, Officer," I say obediently. I feel like a high school slapped on the wrist with detention but not expulsion. My face contorts and twists from utter confusion as I wheel away.

"How could this have happened?" I say aloud to myself, not convinced that I'm not going crazy. I am utterly defenseless.

Perhaps to the officers who stopped me on that beautiful stretch of road, that was the game. It was getting to be an expensive game nonetheless. It left me out of pocket again, and it put another payment into the tip jar of the NYC ticket quota system. Why had they modified the ticket if I was really going at that speed? I wondered who would be the wiser if I wasn't in fact speeding.

The Blacks versus the Yellows

I'm home, staring at the ceiling. I'm feeling deflated and sorry for myself. The people who are set up to protect us are now robbing us. I am a member of the vulnerable and proverbial sheep, protected by the wolves who have wantonly thrown off their sheep's clothing. I feel a sense of broken trust, a subtle but deep pang of violation from being shaken down, with an intuition that things won't ever be the same. I stare at the clock. Same damn day on the road will be here tomorrow.

I am back behind the wheel on a cold early morning. As a first order of business, I pull into a gas station to wash the car, get filled up, put air into the tires, and quickly vacuum the carpeting. The gas station colors are lit up in a glowing green as part of its recognizable brand. I'm a loyal customer because I get discounted prices on gas by using my green gas credit card. I like the meager savings from the card. It offsets my begrudging use of the facilities to keep a relatively clean vehicle in order to stave off bad customer reviews.

Amanda, an aging but athletic-looking woman in her late forties, climbs into the car on Seventieth and East End. She tells me she's running late and asks me to turn down the 1010 WINS news channel as she spreads her bags all over the back seat. I immediately feel on edge and wonder to myself whether Lite FM radio would have been the better choice. She tells me she is running late. Customers mentioning right away that they are running late tend to be anxious, and they tend to give bad reviews if they feel you haven't made the extra effort to get through the traffic lights at a speed fast enough to minimize their morning tardiness.

The morning news does not encourage her already foggy

disposition. A baby has been found thrown in the East River. Kanye has complained again about lack of acclaimed attention at a prestigious music awards ceremony. Upon hearing this on the radio, I laugh to myself.

"Oh, please," blurts Amanda, startling me. "I'm sorry, but that man is so repulsive! I refuse to listen to him anymore. I used to find him a little interesting, but not now. He's so uncivilized and is such a sore loser. I mean, so what if your friend didn't win?" She puts emphasis on the word *friend* in a mocking, deeply derisive tone.

"I mean, so what? Get over it. I went to Wikipedia and actually looked up the difference between best song and best album, and they actually look at the entire album. So what if they figured that overall he wasn't as good? That man is just an asshole!"

I chuckle nervously in mock support.

"I mean, right? Who told him he was God? And that Kardashian? Don't get me started! I mean, no, I don't want to look, nor do I care about, your big, fat, out-of-shape butt! And that Bruce. After a while, it's all too much. I mean, where does it end?"

Her morning vent is coupled by an indignant deepening of the center of her face, where her brows arch in. Her eyes roll, and her lids blink as if the light is unbearable. She shakes her head and stares out the window at the traffic. I drop my eyes and appreciate her honest, raw, cranky rant. As we cross the Manhattan Bridge into Brooklyn, I wonder whether the energy she's consumed to point out her issues with the top entertainment news of the day make it newsworthy material.

I notice a pest in my rearview mirror. A yellow cab is tailgating me in the left center lane. I am to his right but notice his hasty speed. The road runs out ahead of me: a disabled car with its emergency hazard lights flashing and the metallic trunk up, no doubt the cause of the traffic. I attempt to merge to my left, but the cab behind me seizes the opportunity to pass me.

"Hmm, that was rude," I say.

I jerk the steering wheel back into my lane as he passes.

"That *was* rude," she agrees. She huffs an audible breath and blurts out a complaint. "Everyone wants to race. What people don't seem to understand is that they will be at the same spot after you are in a nanosecond. I mean, you were both going the same speed."

I feel the heaviness of her emphasis on the last two words.

Her eyes are again glazed, and she is really angry now. "People driving just don't understand that when the road runs out for the car ahead of them, they should stop and yield to the car ahead of them. It actually slows up traffic when the car ahead of them has to stop and wait. I bet you hate when that happens to you."

"Yeah," I say with a sigh. "It always happens with the yellows."

"I find that the black cars are more courteous than the yellows. It's almost like there's a code among drivers, and the black cars tend to be nicer. Why is that?" she asks.

"Yellow Cabs aren't subject to bad reviews," I say.

"Well, maybe they should be," she sniffs.

I drop her off in a beautiful, tree-lined street on President Street. I admire the rows of neat brownstone townhouses. Brooklyn seems an oasis to me.

The Drivers Code

I drop off a young couple with a new infant at the Metro North station on 125ᵗʰ Street and Park Avenue. I flip the Superlative-issued child booster seat into the trunk of the vehicle. The midafternoon early spring air is cool as I quickly slide back into the warm seat. The seat belt automatically clicks and slides around me as I close the door and turn on the ignition. As I check my mirrors and glide out into the intersection, another black car, a black Suburban sport utility vehicle with T plates, impatiently stalks and tailgates me. I glance at my rearview mirror and notice a shiny, dark-skinned African man with wild, nappy hair and sunglasses waving his arms wildly and pounding on his horn boisterously so that he can get by me. I pound on my horn and raise my arms, thrusting both up excitedly. I always make a point of being a safe space from vehicles, and his vehicle is at an alarmingly close distance from mine. His face resembles some fearless child soldier from somewhere in the African Gold Coast. I'm too tired to care about his impatience.

The African driver pulls up to the red light beside me, gunning the accelerator and staring at me with an icy, murderous expression. I stare back, trying not to notice how the deep scars on his blackened, ashy cheeks and neck contrast with the white, collared shirt he's wearing. I feel my face shake and get warm. Our countenances are still and unrelenting. After four to five seconds of what seem like a terror-filled eternity, he throws his head back and lets into a booming laugh, revealing metallic shining teeth. I laugh too. We both realize the absolute absurdity of our encounter. I feel the tenseness subside from my face. He nods his head at me and purses his thick lips in a way that abruptly ends his laughter, and then he speeds off in front of me up Park Avenue. I wonder whether he is laughing at me or with me. I let out a sigh of relief and make a mental note to avoid any careless confrontation with drivers that escalates to more than a furtive glance of complete and utter indifference.

Time in a Bottle

I stop at a stoplight near Atlantic Avenue in order to head back over the Brooklyn Bridge. I reach into a brown paper bag on the passenger side of my vehicle. I pour three green apples, two bologna sandwiches, and a slice of pound cake onto the seat. It's 5:15 p.m. I watch people drag themselves home and wish I could drive myself home too. I'm getting that isolated feeling again—the feeling I get whenever a sprinkled but lively discussion ends with a departure from the vehicle. Tonight, I'm every bit the affable, entertaining, black city chariot shuffling from place to place in the metropolis. Some conversations that evening with passengers are so compelling that I almost want to park the car and finish the conversation in a neighborhood bar. On some nights like tonight, I become addicted to the discussions, quickly picking up another conversation as one exits. The silence between rides becomes deafening.

I'm underneath the Brooklyn Promenade, roaring toward the bridge. I glance at the Manhattan skyline, and the beautiful lights remind me of the postcards that tourists pick up and peruse from one of those tiny retail spaces left hanging on to survive in Times Square. I finish my meager turkey sandwich dinner and am still hungry, so I make a mental note to stop at the twenty-four-hour McDonald's on Thirty-Fifth Street later tonight. In the back of my mind, this identifies the reason why I'm gaining weight.

I look at my phone. Damn it. My daughter has called me, and I missed it. I would have pulled over to the side of the road just to hear her voice. I didn't pick up to speak to her with a customer inside the car because that would have probably led to a bad review. Now, it's too late to call her back. It's after ten o'clock on a school night, and my ex-wife will have my head on a stick if I try to call now. I feel my heart sink, and my mood changes.

I resign myself to staring at her picture that I have stuffed in the glove compartment for times when she serves as proper motivation to drive. She gets me through the tough days. One glance at her picture fuels me for ten-hour shifts.

Weekends are known to drivers to be more lucrative. The Superlative app frequently broadcasts for drivers to be on the road to take advantage.

I don't take the bait. I spend alternating weekends instead with her. The driving opportunities that the weekends present are unimportant in comparison. I think of the days when I've had too much of the city, and she calls. I drop off the customers, hoping they don't notice my haste. I speed dial her back immediately and couldn't care less about time. I'm happily adrift, suspended with her words that explain her day at school; how she deftly avoids the dangerous, petty girl catfights; and the flirtatious thirteen-year-old boys.

I remember her calling from a strange phone number to report that a school bully had stolen her phone. I dreamed of running the vehicle through the schoolyard to catch the thief who had stolen the day's happiness from her. I was exceptionally filled with rage. But she recognized that I was upset and said she would handle it. By the end of the school day, she was calling me back with her returned phone.

I think about that day. I was willing to give up everything just to see her that very moment. Nothing matters, and certainly not this black vehicle, the leash that pulls me over the five boroughs. Nothing matters at any moment but her. This realization is also when I know that deep down, I hate driving.

It is as if driving keeps me from seeing her. This twisted causation begins to flourish. I'm dead sure I'm not the only divorced person in the labor force who feels this way about putting time in a bottle to save it for their children, to borrow a phrase from the late musician Jim Croce. I think about how it's her unconditional love that fuels the workday, that fuels my vehicle. With the back of my forearm, I wipe away angry tears; in the heavy traffic, I pretend to other drivers that I have something in my eye.

Pound of My Flesh

At home before bed that night, I go over my financial metrics for the day, and I'm gripped by a nagging suspicion that the surge fees are being understated by the company. Superlative, as was explained to me by a manager, claims to strip the surge pricing amount out, separating it from normal mileage billing. Why would they do this? I can't come up with a reason why they would other than to be opportunistic in short-changing the drivers by fiddling with the numbers. Why not declare a percentage from the driver's per daily surge amount? Confused, I shake my head and put down the calculator.

I fare no better in my attempts to calculate my toll fees. E-ZPass, in a letter, has decided to raise the minimum amount that they will take out each month due to "excessive toll activity." I also seem to be getting less toll amounts reimbursed than what is showing on my E-ZPass statement. I can't seem to be able to match the toll amounts deducted from E-ZPass balance to the toll amounts shown as having been reimbursed on my paycheck, because they are from different pay periods; E-ZPass delays the accumulation of toll in the statements. My head starts to hurt as I scratch it, with the thought of more driving just eight hours away. I poke at the television with my remote, terminating the signal with tired eyes. I'm even too exhausted to watch my usual favorite newscasts on Al Jeezera, Press TV, and RT. I prefer these stations because they present the other side of the seedy American narrative pushed at me. (I have a politically well-informed French passenger to thank for the alternate geopolitical narrative.)

I glance over to my slightly dusty, neglected bed table to make sure that my Superlative-issued iPhone will recharge for tomorrow's first three hours. Before long, I will have to plug it in and drive with it in my hands, due to its short power life. It's also because I keep the phone cradle in the front windshield closer to me on the driver side, and the cord is unable to reach the center console where the electric plug-ins are. I wince as I raise myself off of my old couch and head to the dim bedroom of my one-bedroom apartment. On the couch still sits a newspaper open to the article I was reading that said Superlative is the subject of a congressional hearing probing into how their fees are determined. I wonder whether the Taxi and Limousine Commission, the presiding body of all those yellow and green cabs, lobbied to encourage the probe. The hearing investigators accuse Superlative of using a series of price levels to undermine and exploit the driver population by understating the expense side of Superlative's ledger. The price levels, the hearing contended, consists of "usurious" surge pricing, uncompensated toll charges and leasing fees, and "willful but discretionary black car fees," as well as unpaid sales taxes passed on to a wide driver population.

Superlative countered by asserting the use of dynamic pricing through use of a secretive pricing algorithm that was proprietary to the company and therefore not subject to disclosure. Still, something was up that I couldn't put my finger on. I only knew from my struggles that it felt like I was getting screwed. In trying to match my expenses to my driving revenue, I felt more like a driver and less like an accountant. Sure, I went to college and learned what the matching principle was, but I didn't actually know I was to execute it! I wondered whether a new driver from Pakistan would find that question and figure that creating a vast population of underserved laborers who were slaves to the technology would be exactly the business practice of the great, "benevolent" Superlative brand.

I also begin to wonder, *Am I an employee or an independent contractor?*

If I was an independent contractor, then I wouldn't have to pick up a mandatory number of riders within a certain time before being "timed out," as I was cautioned to do virtually. The Superlative policy of termination if there was tip acceptance would be up for discussion too.

All I know is that given my 1099 tax status, I was going to have to itemize like crazy. I was also going to have to accept tips and be vigilant about reporting them.

Nah. Tips? What tips? I think to myself.

I have to get my pound of flesh, no matter my situation. I have to survive.

I'd netted $1,034.00 for the week, so I was okay for the moment. But I was puzzled. My rating went down to a 4.4. Why did my rating go down? I'm always courteous and mindful of the customer. It seems as though people are purposefully but indiscriminately underrating me!

I lie in bed, comfortable but restlessly a moment from sleep. I'm feeling uneasy and resentful. I decide that because a rating below 3.5 would amount to my effective termination, from tomorrow forward, I will only pick up passengers with a 3.5 rating and above. It was only fair. I also will not pick up customers who use a location drop pin instead of an actual physical address. I have long agonized over that stupid pin location causing delays in picking up because the technology malfunctioned. It often led to being in heavy traffic on the wrong side of a bustling avenue. Customers who are either too stupid or too self-important to insert their exact location at pickup will be ruthlessly and unmercifully ignored. I also start to give riders my own harsh ratings for general offenses like obnoxiousness, smoking, rudeness, and vehicle littering. (Many riders treat black car vehicle carpeting like they would a cinema parquet floor.) I come up with a whole host of additional offenses while staring at the ceiling; even failing to greet me with a simple decent hello as a fellow human being offering services is subject to my penalizing scrutiny. I realize that it happens more than I care to pay attention to.

Well, from now on, I think I *will* pay attention. I feel a sense of justifiable empowerment.

Monday Morning Jackasses

I'm heading down a familiar stretch along Fifth Avenue, and I'm pissed off. The passenger in the car, a man easily in his midtwenties, keeps announcing the status of the traffic lights as I try to catch them. "Green light!" he sings obnoxiously whenever I stop to time the traffic lights. His voice is whiny and effeminate, like an unseen mosquito buzzing in my ear. He is anxious, late for an appointment, sitting upright on the edge of the back passenger seat, and leaning in the front passenger space beside my driving space. He is also swiveling his head back and forth, surveying traffic almost in surrogate navigation of the vehicle. I resist the urge to slam on the brakes to send him smashing through the front windshield.

"You can get to the right here. Over! Get over!" he whines.

I ignore him and roll my eyes as other vehicles aggressively scream by us in the morning rush.

My rating has gone back up, and so I figure I can take the hit. I simply don't care. I think about how the rating system terminates drivers with bad ratings while allowing riders with bad ratings to continue to ride, and this seems unreasonable. I want to swing my body around and smash this rider in the face with a clenched fist. I find sudden solace that he's only going to the Chelsea Market Building.

"Okay, green light … Green light! Go!" the rider sings again, leaning forward with a swish of his index finger. My teeth clench now. I have crossed the threshold. I now am in utter contempt of all people whom I don't know and who are still breathing.

Then I get it. It comes to me. New Yorkers are just jackasses on Monday morning.

It's been that kind of a morning anyway, and I'm too tired to care about righting the tone of the day. I've already had to snap at a passenger this morning on the way to JFK Airport who was impatiently tapping his iPhone on the custom wood finishing of the door rests of my vehicle.

"Could you stop fucking doing that to my car?" I scream, startling him. Another hit to my rating earlier, I'm sure.

Then there was the well-dressed Indian man down at Rockefeller Plaza who, after getting out of the car to head inside one of the massive buildings, motioned for me to open the window just to hand me his half-consumed bottle of water. "Could you throw this out for me?"

I winced and couldn't hide my stark incredulity at his lack of courtesy. The fucking jerk couldn't wait five minutes to discard his bottled water into a building lobby trash can, or maybe the small wastebasket underneath the foot of his office desk.

I stop for another traffic light and can't help but think about how I keep forgetting to check the passenger rating before I accept a new ride. I glance down at my Superlative-issued iPhone. I can see why his passenger rating is a 3.1. I really have to start paying closer attention. I again make the promise to myself.

However, starting to cherry-pick my ridership leads to my getting warnings from the Superlative app that I'm cancelling too many rides. I am punitively timed out for ten minutes this morning, disabled by the system, and prompted to log back in because of too many cancellations.

Coming down Houston Street just off of FDR Drive is a mess. There is construction on both sides of the avenue, including the center divide, because the neighborhood has been earmarked for beautification. I make an error in discretion by thinking the car ahead of me can cross the intersection in time before me, and it doesn't. Consequently, I get stuck in the box, which means I'm the idiot in the middle of the intersection when cars and pedestrians start to cross the intersection from the adjacent side. I stare at the steering wheel and feel the looks of derision. A white-haired, deranged-looking, older man in a striped, two-toned, vintage dinner jacket is walking a labradoodle across the street. He wraps the leash between his hands and starts to clap his hands at me in mock applause for my admittedly boneheaded judgment. I nod deeply at him inside the car, cock my arm under my breastplate, and pretend to take a bow. As he passes me and proceeds down the street, I roll down my window.

"Thank you, thank you very much!" I yell. Passersby on the crowded avenue stare at me. I'm both mortified and shocked by my own impulsiveness. I'm the poor sore loser who's stuck in the box. I glance at the car in front of me and notice that one of the stickers has "Ho Lee Chit" prominently displayed on the rear trunk. I raise my eyebrows and wonder if anybody is offended by it.

I've perpetrated countless outbursts, silent and aloud, during the course of the Superlative days and months by now. I curse at drivers who fail to honor the sanctity of moving traffic, drivers who are slow-witted with their three- and four-point turns, and pedestrians who are equally the same with a slothlike road decorum. It is a daily occurrence now to see the shadow of irate raised arms behind me if I don't depress the accelerator quick enough, or drivers with bad or poor judgment who underestimate the dangers of the road by failing to respect the flow of traffic. My eyes set upon a Vision Zero sticker on the passenger side of a black Ford Explorer utility vehicle. Vision Zero is a citywide campaign authored by the city mayor to try to reduce traffic accidents down to zero—a plan that seems well meaning but impossible given the infinite number of crazy-assed drivers.

Haste Makes Waste

I t's early morning, and I'm on Grand Central Parkway, heading back from a short run to LaGuardia Airport. Something doesn't seem right. The traffic seems hasty. Haste always makes waste, as the expression goes. The traffic is tight going back toward the city, but vehicles are screaming toward their gaps in traffic, only to stop short or yield to other drivers taking more risk by accelerating harder toward the gaps in front of them. This causes the traffic to be choppy and not cohesively flowing. My mental defensive shield goes up.

I think about my first driving instructor, a self-proclaimed "professional driving instructor." He was an intense but grizzled, stern Hispanic man in his sixties wearing a Depression-era po'boy styled cap. I remember that he cautioned me to pull over to the side of the road and waggled a finger at me, ensuring that I'd never forget the verbal warning. "Listen to me, okay? Look at traffic and observe the road. Always scan the road in front of you and behind you. Anticipate. Use your eyes and your feet. Watch for transgressors of the number one rule, which is never disrupt the even flow, the speed, of traffic. You can see them, the drivers who make the slow three-point U-turn in traffic, disrupting oncoming cars both ways. The driver who decides to unwisely park on the corner of a busy turning intersection. The driver who has slow senses and doesn't properly accelerate and match speeds with the other vehicles when merging or changing lanes. Drivers with bad or poor judgment who underestimate the dangers of traffic. Drivers are not to be trusted. They are careless all the time, even reckless. You can always tell that by how they control or treat the speed and space in between them and the next car. Sometimes they totally ignore it. You see, you can feel the car in front of you. When he slows down, you slow down. When you see those red stopping lights flash, you stop. When you see a driver risk an accident by increasing the speed between the gaps in vehicles just to stop at the next light, you know you should avoid that driver. That driver is an accident waiting to happen. It's simply a matter of time before the percentages catch up to that driver, and that driver has an accident. Everybody wants to be first, but when it's time to pay the piper, someone has to pay for being hasty. And haste makes waste."

He raised his voice an octave at the driving commandment. "What causes accidents? I'll tell you. The lack of awareness and consideration of other drivers. When you see drivers on the road after an accident, don't feel bad for them. I don't. I honestly don't feel bad for drivers who get into an accident, because they are always thinking that what they're doing and where they're going is more important than everyone else. Even if they notice an overly aggressive driver, someone will have to yield. If nobody yields, that will always be a recipe for danger and disaster. Think about Princess Diana's driver. Now, that guy was a real prick."

I abruptly sensed that the "professional driver" had a thing for Princess Diana.

The Don of Digital

"**M**an, I was spoiled by Google out West in Silicon Valley." Kyeong is a Korean software engineer flying to Boston to work for an "app startup." Young and smart, he sports expensive Lacoste glasses and sinks back into the back passenger seat in dark jeans and a navy Massachusetts Institute of Technology T-shirt. "I seriously will not work for anyone unless they have amazing perks, and this place is just ridiculously good." He beams. He is calm, focused, and unapologetically entitled, clearing enjoying being on the right side of a tight employment market. I wonder if his success was the result of a disciplined, well-thought-out path of difficult computer science curricula and Ramen noodles. He goes on to further explain the allure of the "highly nontraditional" office space layout: basketball gym attached, ping-pong, and yards-long, pillow-filled swinging couches for afternoon naps. All meals are free. There is a free laundry service and free home cleaning. The theory is that if everything is taken care of at home, employees will stay at work with no need to go home.

I surmise that the practice works. He can barely wait to get there once I take his bags out of the trunk and drop them unto the departure sidewalk at LaGuardia.

The Knowledge Meets the NYC Tip Jar

I'm headed to a swanky hotel on Ludlow Street, the one that always has yellow taxis and luxury black cars in front of it, off-loading baggage and hipster passengers from far-flung cities. I see the usual suspects from the black car companies: Mega, Diplo, Dial Seven, Seaman, Superlative.

My current passengers are a young couple from London. I can smell the money on them. We spend the first several minutes of the ride to JFK Airport over the Manhattan Bridge in abject silence. They are perhaps in mourning of the trip already, or simply relieved to be on a Superlative car headed to the airport to catch their flight.

"Temperature okay in the car?"

"Yes, thank you," the young woman says in a perfectly polite, royal-like accent. I ask them if they managed to see all the sights. The Broadway shows were nice, and so was the wedding at the Grand Prospect Hall in Prospect Park, Brooklyn.

"Ah," I say in recognition, but really not giving a fuck.

Minutes pass. Then we hit traffic in Brooklyn. Very heavy traffic. My GPS, mounted in the windshield on the driver side, begins to flash red along the intended route. We crawl along for fifteen minutes at barely a runner's pace. I see worried looks in the rearview mirror.

"Are we making good time for your flight?" I ask, spitting out the well-rehearsed line.

"Well, I'm not exactly sure. Um, Could you find some way to get us off of this?"

Shit. Now, my internal alarm goes off.

It has started to drizzle very hard, and large, tall box trucks and tankers limit my visibility through the windshield wipers. I signal and merge the car hard into a left lane while a bespectacled lady looks at her cellphone. I turn off of the busy street, figuring that the GPS will just recalculate.

Flashing lights beckon me over to the right.

My heart sinks into the bottom of my stomach. Shit. I'm being pulled over again. This time with a customer in the car.

"We're being stopped by the cops?" the young English lady says to the Englishman.

"I'm afraid so." I apologize to the couple as the policeman approaches.

"No, no. No worries about it," the man says.

"Please, please, s'all right," the woman says.

"Do you realize that you made an illegal left turn? License and registration," the officer says.

I speed as fast as I can legally go without getting another ticket to JFK Airport, apologizing profusely along the way every ten minutes. My brow sweats. "I really can't believe this, folks. I'm so sorry."

I picture my driver rating going straight down to hell. I dance and jive my way to the trunk of my car to set their luggage down quickly and gingerly onto the airport sidewalk.

In the end, the couple laugh and consider it part of the "New York experience."

"How much was the fine for the violation?" the man asks, his voice raising an octave higher at the end of the sentence like an accuser.

"One hundred fifteen bucks," I sigh.

He peels off seven twenties and hands them to me. I feel like falling to my knees and emoting tearful appreciation. My expense budget would've been wrecked. I climb back behind the wheel and close my eyes, alarmed by a damning realization.

I have nine points on my license in a span of a little over seven months.

Superlative Bubble

The full-scale recognition of my plight hits me as I sit in a warm bubble bath. The bath is towering with bubbles, soothing my aching muscles of the backs of my arms and consoling my anxiety. It's obvious that all the business with Superlative will come to an end soon. This is considering my tangles with the New York City Parking Violations Bureau and the Taxi and Limousine Commission. I've made my peace with this.

The bubbles are plentiful and luxurious. The bathwater's sensation varies in delicious warmth as I shift my tired body parts among the dark blue hue. I sink into the bath, slide down on the smoothness of the porcelain, and close my eyes, listening to the popping sounds as each bubble extinguishes itself. There are so many of them, an overwhelming endless legion of bubbles. I close my eyes, and the popping becomes a symphony to my ears.

I find myself in a strange, melancholy mood, and I let the mood just wash over me. One bath within another. I hear the faintness of a dog bark in the distance outside the small window of the small bathroom. Then I hear the faint sounds of an endless parade of vehicles careening down the avenue outside the building. A siren wails. I close my eyes in deep relaxation for a good while.

I awaken out of my relaxed trance twenty-five minutes later. The mountains of bubbles in the bath are gone, replaced by a slick formation of tiny bubbles. The sounds of the popping are very faint now. I can still see the tiny bubbles, each one flickering off in its own impending order of time. The tower of luxurious bubbles that was caressing my ears is gone. The water has cooled considerably. I am lukewarm, still comfortable but not as much as before. The water has lost its blue hue and becomes colder when I shift my legs. I sit up in a supine position with my head in my hands and my elbows on top of my extended knees. I think about my own short, tenuous existence.

I think about time.

How will my bubble go pop? Will it be under the calamitous stress of another bubble? Or will it be in open water, flickering out like a soft night-light? Did some of the bubbles that were on top of other subordinate bubbles cause them stress and hasten their popping? I couldn't know. I only know that if I gaze long enough, the bubbles begin to look like the countless lights of cities reflecting onto the water. I stare at one microscopic bubble and wait for it to extinguish. After a minute and a half, it doesn't. It figures. As the saying goes, a watched pot never boils. I rise and step out of the bath, breaking my oath to see each bubble through to the end.

So much for life's promises.

Life, Sports, and the Thirteenth

I'm in a good mood this early morning because my first trip is out to New Jersey, which means I get relief from the morning rush hour. I'm always happy about drives out of the city; they countertrend the long, snaking traffic coming into the city. I make my way downtown along the West Side Highway toward the Holland Tunnel. I enjoy twisting along that artery that outlines the western edge of the island, down past the large Golf sign above the Chelsea Piers Sport Complex on Twenty-first Street. The traffic is surprisingly light as I see Freedom Tower glistening in the distance like a silver falcon.

We enter and exit the Holland Tunnel, and my busy passenger fields some important morning calls, on which I enjoy eavesdropping. I turn the FM Lite music down to accommodate him. He is advising a client about some sort of employment compensation, I think. He is confident and reassuring, and his responses are calm and automatic, like an old song he's heard too many times. Perhaps he used to enjoy singing the song, but now it's the song that endears him to his targeted audience.

I think of a recording pop star announcing to her disappointed audience that she'll no longer be singing the song that made her a star. She's sick from singing it. Should she have been allowed to reach such a lofty position in the face of all the obscure singers yet to find their audience? Has the pop star lost perspective in a world where that kind of luck is hard to come by? What if the pop star suddenly lost everything? Would she have a change of heart about singing her heart out again?

The drive into the Woodlands of New Jersey will thankfully be a long one. My aggregate percentage take will be fractionally higher, which suits me fine. The passenger, a portly man in his midfifties with a neatly trimmed beard, closes his laptop and searches my face in the rearview mirror. He's wearing an expensive but slightly oversized navy suit, and I noticed his black wingtip shoes when he loaded his small neat black luggage with the Swiss army knife insignia into the trunk. He snatches off circular, tortoise-shelled spectacles from his round, reddish, sunburned face.

"This will be quite a long ride today," he announces.

"Yep," I say back.

His tone is polite but cold and ambivalent, and it's especially noticeable when he responds to my usual question concerning the temperature of the car. "It's fine, thank you."

He surveys his tablet, checking the probable endless e-mails. "Can I make use of your recharging port?" he asks, extending a wire to me.

"Sure, no problem," I say, not missing a beat. I evade a large tractor trailer and merge into the center lane.

"Good to be done with morning calls and face this lovely day," he says. He says it as if a heavy load has been lifted off of his shoulders.

"Yeah, it's a beauty," I say.

"You're not originally from New York City," he says. He extends a fat, pinkish index finger as if pinning me to a wall.

"Nope, 'fraid not," I say.

"Whereabouts?"

"Upstate New York."

He nods silently and stares at the lushness of the trees along the expressway. I glance serenely at them too.

"May I take a guess at what you do?" I ask him. "It's kind of a game that I like to play with myself when I hear business calls, and to pass the time while driving."

"Okay, sure. G'head, shoot."

"You're a lawyer specializing in executive compensation," I blurt out.

"Female executive compensation. But not me—my partner. I do mostly labor contracts. I do ERISA, the Employee Retirement Income ... er, I do cases that involve employee benefit plans."

I detect and appreciate the simplification. "I was that close." I hold out my thumb with my index finger.

"Yeah, pretty close. So what's a guy like you doing in a gig like this? Actor?"

"Naw, I'm between jobs, doing this until the next thing comes along." I'm shocked by my complete honesty. I usually like to hedge the answer with a self-conscious lie.

"Nothing wrong with taking stock of where you are," he says. "Sometimes I wonder about lawyering. I'd like to marshal a nice boat around the tropics. Perhaps open a bar. Maybe soon enough."

"That sounds pretty awesome," I add.

We talk about a lot of things during the long drive: the stressful frenetic pace of the city, the seemingly declining standards of decency and civilization, Snowden, Monsanto, the Keystone pipeline, Netanyahu, supply side economics.

"Trickle-down economics is a hoax," he opines. "It's a bait-and-switch confidence game where the upper class promises to create jobs but horde resources instead by using foreign tax havens and equity stock buybacks to preserve wealth." These conversations are mostly him rambling on seemingly with no filter. I pepper his grand monologues with varying encouraging acknowledgments, like the bartender of a drunken but grandiose customer.

We talk about refugees, and the Trans Pacific Partnership (TTIP) that President Obama champions. The topic of the nuclear family and siblings comes up.

"Funny we should be on the subject. I'm actually on my way to my eldest daughter's house. She's getting a divorce."

"I'm sorry to hear that," I say in consolation.

"Nah, it's really okay. Things have not been quite right in her household for some time now. I told her if things got unbearable for her and she makes the decision to divorce, I would support her. It was tough staying out of it for so long and watching her. Once she'd made the decision to sell the house, I told her she can come home. I actually live in Florida. I consider myself very lucky. I live in a gated community, and my life is relatively easy. I can't tell you what it must be like or feel like to be an African American male in this country. I can tell you I'd probably be pretty wound up. My community is pretty unwelcoming for ethnic groups as a whole. Where I live, I can easily go a couple of days without seeing people of color, unless they are delivering something or coming in as a nanny or something like that."

His eyes drop in deliberative thought. "Even in some of the companies I represent, people of color on the corporate counsel floor are literally nowhere to be found. I mean, the token joke in most corporate offices inherently presumes that there isn't even remotely a fair amount of ethnicity or diversity in corporate offices. It's a pretty sad reality, actually. I think it all boils down to, and has always boiled down to, how resources are consumed in private communities pretty much all over this country ... and which families from generation to generation get to consume the lion's share of those resources, whether we're talking about cotton or natural gas. I can't imagine what it must be like to wake up every day in this country as a person of color, with that reality over my head."

"There's always sports and entertainment," I joke.

We both nod and then shake our heads.

"Sports should definitely resemble the real world—pure, unadulterated meritocracy. But you can see that beginning to be racially tainted too nowadays. Little League World Series, and so forth. You just have a feeling that the best performing kids are not the ones shown on ESPN. My wife always asks me why sports salaries are so high, and I tell her because it's based on a skill set that defies bias." He snorts and waggles a fat pink index finger.

"A black colleague in our office does constitutional amendment issues. If I were a person of color, I'd be really pissed and concerned about the thirteenth amendment to the constitution. I mean, it basically funnels black people back into subjective slavery. Now, I honestly don't know of any meaningful minority employment in my firm of three hundred lawyers worldwide, but just imagine, for the sake of argument, if that sentiment was extrapolated to other respective industries—which wouldn't be too far stretched from reality, okay? That means government employment could pretty much make up the lion's share of black and Latino or non-white, upwardly mobile people as an alternative, right? So when my party says we want to shrink government, what could that mean? Indirectly forcing more people back into that funnel, perhaps? You know, being white sometimes is like watching generation after generation of thoroughbreds drink from a trough that excludes any other kind of horse from drinking. Would I would do is, I would dismantle the thirteenth amendment and decouple it from any labor standard. Now, hear me out. Being incarcerated has nothing to do with working for free. You want them to work? Then pay them so that they get to support their families, even if they happen to be in prison—where they were funneled in the first place indirectly from lack of opportunity." He smacks his lips as he finishes and smiles with a satisfied, magnanimous expression.

"Well, that does make sense. I appreciate your candor." That is all I could say as we pull into what can be described as the circular driveway of a obscenely massive estate.

Paid Forward

My balance in my checking account will be negative for the next day or so. I do the only thing I can think of to get this off of my mind: I drive. I drive to combat being financially in the negative, and what that means in America is that I am one of a countless number of people in America whose wages are not keeping up with inflationary pressures.

It is the dead of night shift, well past two o'clock in the morning. The streets are desolate and peaceful. The rides are less hectic and of low stress: trendy clubs, late restaurant table reservations, exhausted people returning home from late shifts or partying hard, burning the candle at both ends of ambitious careers. They are typically too tired to be particular about how they get home. Most times they are half asleep, and they have to prompted to awaken from a dreary nap when we've reached their residence.

I find myself again over the beautiful lights of the Brooklyn Bridge, speeding toward trendy Fort Greene and having a conversation with Charlene, a short-haired soccer mom who recounts a tale about finding an expensive Stradivarius in a yellow cab that she'd sat in one afternoon. The case of the instrument denoted that it belonged to a Julliard student. Classical music lover that she is, she immediately instructed the yellow cabbie to speed hastily toward Julliard in search of the student. She found the music student some minutes later, a transplant from Oklahoma sobbing on the steps of the school over the lost instrument. The student was ecstatically pleased to find Charlene stepping out of the yellow cab with the cherished instrument in her outstretched hands.

We talk about karma and her unique interpretation of it. She talks about how things should be paid forward, like the movie, to even out the wrinkles that always seem to occur in the universe.

"No good deed should go unpunished," she laments.

I provide a story, given to me by an attractive, dark-haired, young Brooklyn girl originally from Uzbekistan who was continually harassed by a Muslim driver for seeming too secular and not engaging more intensively in the Islamic faith.

"Wow. He should be reported for harassment and fired. I find burqas particularly disturbing," she says.

"Really? Why, may I ask?" I say.

"Because the donning of a burqa is not about the woman," she explains with a tilt of a penciled eyebrow. "It's about the males of that culture not being able to deal with and exercise their own self-control sexually. They oppress the woman in that culture to compensate."

"Hmm, that's an interesting take," I muse.

We ride in silence, allowing the weight of her observation to take hold.

"By the way, did you hear about the CEO of Superlative?" she goes on, still raising that penciled eyebrow.

"What, the hearing they made him go to?"

"No, no. Apparently he's quite a megalomaniac. He ordered the private investigations of financial journalists who say anything negative about the company."

"Wow," I say, not really concerned about the subject.

"Yeah, he's a Kiwi too. I married a Kiwi once. They're crazy," she says with an emphatic wink and a nod. "It's also quite natural for someone with recently acquired super wealth to become just as bad as the ones who've been that way since they were born with silver spoons."

"Born which way?" I ask.

"Born with a taste for authority," she says, batting her fabulous, false eyelashes.

The gesture is timed perfectly. She climbs out of the car as if it were her own royal chariot, into the open air of an eerily quiet, beautiful, tree-lined block of Pacific Street. She hustles into a gated brownstone, activating a bright automatic flood lamp.

Yellows Are Burning

I'm sitting in front of the Graybar Building connected to Grand Central Station on Forty-First Street and Lexington Avenue. I think about the two-hundred-dollar assessment levied to me by the Taxi and Limousine Commission. This is an annual penalty for the points I have outstanding on my hack license. The spidery tentacles of the Department of Motor Vehicles and the TLC have me on edge. I feel like a helpless housefly trying to detach from a sticky, lethal roll of flypaper attached to the ceiling. The more I move to try to detach myself, the more tangled I get. My driver's instinct alerts me that I'm in a tricky spot because Lexington Avenue can get ridiculously gridlocked. I have the momentary solace of being out of the way and relatively invisible.

Someone standing in the street raps thick knuckles on the window of the passenger side, smudging the window. I swing around, wondering what the reason is for that action. The person who struck the window, a thin, gaunt man in his fifties, points toward the direction of the street behind me and rushes off.

I swing my head around to the street to find adjacent to me a yellow cab with the interior almost completely engulfed in flames. It's apparent also that the driver has left the vehicle and is long gone. I quickly jump up in my seat, turn on the ignition, and shift hard into reverse down to the end of the block. Police action initializes to block off the street, with officers waving their arms frantically over their heads to stop traffic, and fire sirens approach in the distance.

People stop and stare at the smoldering spectacle of the yellow cab, which is now fully in flames. Some even take videos with their smartphones. The chassis of the vehicle starts to strip away, and it crackles and pops. A small explosion occurs, and a "Wooo" sound emits from pursed lips of the crowd of onlookers, as if enjoying some Fire Island fireworks display. I enjoy the spectacle too, whipping out my phone and recording the inferno. I silently anticipate the next little explosion, but it never comes, and the fire department races through.

I figure that my next passenger has been held up in the Graybar Building as a result. But there seems to be something metaphorically foreboding about sitting here and recording the destruction of the yellow cab, and what ridesharing technology will ultimately do to the medallion yellow cab industry.

Between a Rock and a Hard Place

My young teenage daughter is in tow this morning, and I'm running late. I make that turn on 217th Street and Marble Hill Avenue, where I see the street sign: "No left turn between 7:00 a.m. and 8:30 a.m." There is a red slash prominently slicing through the black and white lettering. *It's still not yet seven in the morning,* I say to myself. I turn the wheel hand over hand, make the left, and prepare to step on the accelerator to go straight through toward the Broadway Bridge when I see a sight in my rearview mirror that is absolutely the last thing I would want to see:

The flashing lights of a black unmarked Dodge Charger police vehicle with deeply tinted windows, hailing me to stop. I apply the brakes, immediately slap both hands hard to my forehead several times, and scream, "No! No! No!"

This startles my daughter, and her wide eyes search mine with angst.

"I'm sorry, Pie. I didn't mean to scare you," I say. I cradle my head with both hands.

"What's wrong, Daddy?" she asks.

"I'm being stopped—again!" I mutter, staring into the windshield in disbelief.

"But I thought we had the time to get through ..."

"I thought so too, Pie," I answer. We sit for what seems like forever as the officer sits in his vehicle, waiting to approach.

I drop my daughter off late for school on Ninety-Fifth Street and West End Avenue. I roar down to the Ninety-Sixth street exit for a brief reprieve in the small parking lot of the red clay tennis courts along the West Side Highway. This is the daytime taxi graveyard, similar to the New York City teachers' rubber room for burned-out educators. The cabby burnouts are parked everywhere, some sticking socked feet out of open car doors and windows while sleeping off the exhaustive burden of late shifts. Some drivers sit behind the wheel, staring blankly out over the burgundy of the red clay tennis courts and out into the West River, contemplating something deliberative. A square-jawed, black Dominican driver from Mega, an uptown Dominican-owned livery company, is slumped over the steering wheel, holding it as if clutching a pillow while he sleeps. Another older Eastern European black car driver in a late model luxury Mercedes Benz is smashing the dust out of floor mats while being dressed impeccably. He becomes irritated as dust settles on his black suede loafers. Another disheveled yellow cabbie, door ajar due to lack of air conditioning, sits doing the *Daily News* crossword puzzle. He feverishly scratches his shaved head.

I sit staring at the steering wheel and the Hudson River. In a few days, the TLC will be generating a suspension request of my hack license. I think about how I will be required to defend myself in a court hearing. I think about the fact that if I don't prevail in the upcoming hearing, my driving privileges will be irrevocably suspended. I think for an inordinately long time about how I allowed the situation to occur. I am between a rock and a very hard place, with no place to turn.

I head toward the streets again, feeling like I have nothing to gain and everything to lose. I pass a familiar figure, his unshaven face up in the seat of his yellow cab, mouth open and snoring in the sun. It's Kent. I smile with a sudden sadness, silently wish him well, and say goodbye to him in my mind. I'm too ashamed to wake him and seek commiseration.

Flipping Off a Cop

I pick up a fare going east on Ninety-Sixth Street to make my way to LaGuardia Airport. Michael is a musician going to play a music festival in Los Angeles, the city of angels. While I hear him on the phone with his agent turning down a studio gig, police sirens sound in the short distance. I strain my neck to make out the general direction of them. My upcoming Taxi and Limousine Commission suspension hearing looms heavy on my mind. Traffic officers are directing vehicles unto the FDR ramp. The sirens soon make themselves known as two undercover police vehicles race past us in the opposite direction. Horns honk before I can even touch the accelerator with my right foot. A traffic officer emerges out of nowhere to shout inside the open window of my vehicle startling me. "Come on, come on! Move along!

In what I can only describe as a startled reaction, the middle finger of my left hand shoots out and slaps itself against the window adjacent to him.

The traffic cop, a tall African American man with high cheekbone features and a neatly pressed uniform, seems surprised by my reaction to him. His eyes bulge out of the sockets. I step on the gas hard, speed away, and whirl around the half circle unto the FDR north ramp.

"Dude, did you just flip off a traffic cop?" Michael asks, taking his phone off of his ear.

"Force of habit," I declare, surprised by the frankness of my response. It is the last act of a desperate man.

"Haste Makes Waste" Meets the Tip Jar

Across from the Bronx Botanical Gardens on Fordham Road is a nondescript white commercial building that houses the Department of Motor Vehicles. I sit waiting in one of the small hearing rooms that serve as an administrative courtroom for moving traffic violations. I shuffle uneasily in the first row of seats, awaiting my DMV hearing. In the small courtroom, I survey the room and see the usual officers of the court: an administrative judge, a bailiff, and a court secretary busily typing a transcript of courtroom events. A traffic court lawyer, a large, barrel-chested Latino, holds a stack of tickets and gestures to an older Hispanic woman with disheveled, stringy dark hair.

The judge, a youthful but balding man in his thirties, calls out her name. "Miss Escovedo?" the judge motions.

The woman cautiously approaches the bench.

The traffic court lawyer stands beside the judge's bench and leans into the judge for a short conference. He casually shuffles the stack of tickets like a deck of playing cards while they exchange whispering tones. The case is dismissed, and the lawyer gestures for them to exit the courtroom.

"Docket number zero zero five eight six seven two four, City of New York versus ..." My last name is shouted aloud by the bailiff, alerting me.

"Presiding Officer Petrone," the judge calls, and the officer approaches the bench seemingly out of nowhere. He was seated to the far side of the judge's bench, and I'd missed him. As a surprise to me, he is also clean shaven. I can feel my pulse rate quicken and my face tremble. He is a broad-shouldered Italian man in his late twenties, with an unshaven shadow on his face. He clasps a stack of tickets, and he begins to recite the charges against me.

"Good morning, Judge. Officer Petrone, shield number five eight three six seven three seven six. Subject was observed making an illegal left turn not in accordance with the posted sign on the corner of …"

My mind wanders during his recital of the moving violation. I stare at his black motorcycle boots until I'm startled by the mention of my name again.

"You are charged with violation of section 453 of the New York City traffic penal code. How do you plead?"

"Not guilty," I protest, clearing my throat.

"Defendant has pleaded not guilty for the record." The judge sniffs summarily, glancing at the court secretary.

"Do you have any questions to ask of the officer that might be material to this disposition?"

"Good morning. Um, yes, Judge, I do," I stammer.

"You can proceed when you're ready."

"Thank you, Judge." I turn my attention to the officer. "Officer, were you aware of the time that you pulled me over?" I ask accusingly.

"Yes," the officer snaps quickly.

"What time was that?"

"That time is stated on the ticket," the officer snorts.

"Officer, you stopped me, and then you walked back to your vehicle. Are you aware of how long you spent in your vehicle?"

The officer purses his lips arrogantly. "I don't know …"

"What's your point?" the judge interjects.

"Your Honor, he stopped me before the time that was posted on the signpost, and then he made me wait into the period of violation that was shown on the sign!"

"Okay, that's allowable. Answer the question," the judge continues.

"I don't have an estimation of the time I was checking his plate," Officer Petrone says, searching his notes.

"No, not the time you checked the plates. The total time you waited for the time on the sign to kick in," I interrupt.

"Hang on, he responded," the judge warns me.

"But Your Honor!"

"All right, we've noted your point. Do you have any other questions for the officer?"

"Uh, yes. I have one more point to make," I say, pulling out another ticket from my shirt pocket.

"What's this?" bellows the judge.

"This is another ticket I got before." My face wells up with desperation. "Judge I'm showing you this ticket because if you'll look closely, the ticket the officer filled out is not as complete as this one. I mean, look at how quickly and sloppily the officer's ticket is written compared to this one!"

"Hang on, sir," the judge interrupts me. "Why are you showing me another ticket other than the one in question today?"

My face feels warm as I continue. I think to myself how things are veering away from how I had planned. "Judge, I thought I'd show you this to suggest strongly to you that the officer sloppily filled out the ticket because I was actually in time going through the school zone. He did it quickly and sloppily just to raise his ticket revenues. He was just trying to get in the last ticket!" My voice cracks with nervous indignation.

"So you're showing me another ticket? Don't show me any tickets other than the one we're discussing today," the judge snaps. He turns to the administrative clerk. "Print out the ticket in question, please, Pearl."

The clerk taps a few strokes on a keyboard, and a copy of a ticket whirs out of a printer.

"That's three points," says the judge.

"No, it's two points," I whine, surprised by my quick, defensive retort in front of His Holiness.

"Pearl, could you check the points?" snaps the judge.

The clerk swiftly taps on keys and peers at the screen. "Two points," she says.

I hold my breath, secretly celebrating my small victory.

"You have already eight outstanding points," the judge growls, swinging the screen toward himself and pressing a hairy knuckle against the screen. I feel my fate being sealed. So much for referring to more than the ticket in question.

"Is that it with your questions before I decide the verdict?"

"Yes, Judge," I quip.

"All right. The State of New York finds you guilty in this matter of—"

"Wait, but excuse me, Judge. You heard him say that he didn't know what time it was when he went to his car after pulling me over."

"I have made that determination. Don't interrupt this proceeding. You could face another surcharge for disruption of this hearing!" the judge growls. "Now, the State of New York finds you guilty and in violation of your points obligation. You will be directed to pay a penalty surcharge of two hundred seventy-five dollars. You'll find the cashier's window outside and down the hall."

My mouth drops open. I am floored by the lack of merit given to my argument and the inherent alliance between the officer and the presiding judge. I snatch up my bag and storm outside, ignoring the plexiglass cashier window on the way out. Fuming and completely depleted of air, I push into the bathroom doors in the hallway.

In the dimly lit, dingy, white-walled confines of the bathroom I press the faucet for cold water and cup lukewarm water over my face with both hands. I lean forward and down, letting the water cascade over my head and down my cheeks. I feel my chest tighten with stress, and my mood is sullen. The water stings my eyes, and I don't notice the officer come in pushing aggressively through the bathroom door. His expression is of a smirk after a dirty joke.

"You try to make me look incompetent in court in front of that judge? Nice try, nigger. All you nigger drivers are a fuckin' dime a dozen," he says. He spits into the sink in front of him and doesn't look at me directly. He stares narcissistically at himself into a cracked mirror and leans on the sink, studying a blemish above his lip. He dabs at it with a tissue and then tosses the tissue angrily into the wastebasket.

"I would say better luck next time, nigger, but there won't be a next time, will there?"

I'm frozen, paralyzed in silence, with my face over the sink dripping with water. I stare at his holster and I notice the top strap has been loosened. I don't move a muscle. He represents the law, heavy-handed, confronting and challenging me. I turn my face away from him, and he leaves as quickly as he entered, like a subsiding shadow. I close my eyes, breathe out heavily, and reach for a paper towel.

I trudge out into the hallway, where I see him make a quick left farther down the hall and back into the courtroom. I push out into the street, and blood and sunlight rushes to my face. I think about marching back into the courtroom building to explain to the judge what has just transpired, but doubt overwhelms me.

A city bus hurls by with an advertisement on the back: "Working for Superlative means having the freedom to work when I want."

I walk briskly toward the parking lot, heading back to my vehicle. Police officers mill around as they take turns attending hearings, condemning the accused. I see the familiar black Dodge Charger muscle car of the undercover officer gleaming in the sun, attended to by two hired transients down on their luck, seeking lunch money for the day. One, a particularly dark African, leans over a bucket clouded by soap suds, dreads falling to the sides of his shoulders. In my excitable mind, the entire scenario seems exploitative of slaves on an oppressive concrete plantation searing in the sun.

My face is flush and my ears are burning. I spot a good-sized red brick underneath the lining of the parking lot fence. My thoughts go wildly where they will, now white hot with rage. I kneel, reach out for the brick, and dislodge it from underneath the parking lot fence with a tug. Like a baseball outfielder retrieving a ball at the bottom of the fence in the outfield, I whirl around, take several pivot steps, and hurl the heavy red brick into the windshield of the officer's vehicle, the black Dodge Charger. The transients scamper away on their knees. I'm numb, and my eyes are red and affixed. I must look like a complete madman. My mind, overcooked with rage, shuts down as police shout, pointing and rushing toward me with hostile expressions.

Epilogue

I am standing on the corner of 228th Street and Marble Hill Avenue, across from the Methodist church, six months later. I stand here contemplative and incredulous, glaring across the street because the sign that I allegedly failed to obey two months and six months ago has been removed and replaced by two "Do Not Enter" signs on both sides of the street. I think about the reasoning behind the removal of the original restrictive sign that finally doomed me as a black car driver, but what does it matter now? Somehow, it was deemed that the sign is now unfit to stand. It is not there anymore. I think about the quiet six months of a year's misdemeanor sentence for destruction of the officer's property that I underwent at the Anna M. Kross Correctional Center at Rikers Island. My temporary loss of good sense was given some consideration, along with the officer having a relative degree of questionable behavior on his record historically toward minorities. (The officer was ordered to undergo racial sensitivity training.) I had anger management classes alongside husbands who assaulted and abused their wives. One particular client burned his wife with hot lye. In the classes, the decision I made to fly into a blind rage was analyzed and picked apart for my instructive purposes over and over again, until that past decision makes a pit form in my stomach with every afterthought.

I drink from the cup of experience and swallow the bitter pill of regret.

But for now, my mind wrestles with the absence of the street sign that brought my employment to a screeching halt. I am remiss and sorely disappointed that the sign is not there to scoff at.

I smile and muse to myself about all the people I have spoken to, the things I've witnessed during my Superlative experience, and the countless faces that make up the big city. I think of faces in hundreds of other cities just like this one. I shove my hands deep in my jean pockets and head toward the BX10 bus stop, toward the temporary shelter that I now call home. I will rise tomorrow morning to see my youngest daughter, my ray of sunshine, off to school. My other daughter is off to college, awaiting a visit. They both will see me rise again, and with my hopes, they'll be ever mindful of their own search for a qualitative existence and an enduring legacy of self-determination.

Printed in the United States
By Bookmasters